The Return

of the

caravels

The Return
of the
caravels

A Novel

António Lobo Antunes

Translated from the portuguese
by Gregory Rabassa

Grove press / New York

Originally published in Portuguese under the title *As Naus,* by Publicações Dom Quixote, Lisbon

Published simultaneously in Canada
Printed in the United States

FIRST EDITION

Library of Congress Cataloging-in-Publication Data
Antunes, António Lobo, 1942–
[Naus. English]
The return of the caravels: a novel / António Lobo Antunes ; translated from the Portuguese by Gregory Rabassa.
p. cm.
ISBN 0-8021-1708-2
I. Rabassa, Gregory.   II. Title.
PQ9263.N77 N3813 2002
869.3'42—dc21   2001051236

DESIGN BY LAURA HAMMOND HOUGH

Grove Press
841 Broadway
New York, NY 10003

02 03 04 05   10 9 8 7 6 5 4 3 2 1

Dedicated to

Nelson de Matos

The Return

of the

caravels

He'd passed through Lixbon eighteen or twenty years earlier on the way to Angola and what he remembered best were his parents' rooms in the boardinghouse on Conde Redondo where they were staying in the midst of a clatter of pots and women's exasperated grumbling. He recalled the communal bathroom, a washbasin with a set of baroque faucets in imitation of fish that vomited out sobs of brownish water through their open gills, and the time he came upon a man on in years smiling on the toilet with his pants down around his knees. At night the window would be open and he'd see the illuminated Chinese restaurants, the sleepwalking glaciers of electrical-appliance stores in the shadows, and blond heads of hair above the paving stones of the sidewalks. So he'd wet his bed because he was afraid of finding the smiling gentleman beyond the rusty fish or the blond heads of hair that dragged clerks along the corridor, twirling room keys on their pinkies. And he'd end up falling asleep with dreams of the endless streets of Coruche, the twin lemon trees in the prior's grove, and his blind grandfather, with blank statue eyes, sitting on a bench by the tavern door as a flock of ambulances wailed along Gomes Freire on their way to São José Hospital.

On the day we sailed, going through a narrow street with the residences of demented countesses, the shops of hallucinated bird dealers, and tourist bars where the English went for their morning gin transfusion, the taxi dropped us off beside the Tagus on a strip of sand called Belém, according to what could be read on the nearby train stop with a scale on one side and a urinal on the other, and he caught sight of hundreds of people and teams of oxen that were bringing stone blocks for a huge building, led by squires in scarlet habits, indifferent to the taxis, the vans with American divorcées and Spanish priests and the nearsighted Japanese who were taking pictures of everything, chatting in their sharp-beaked samurai tongue. Then we put our baggage on the ground beyond the agapanthuses that mechanical sprinklers were aspersing with circular spurts, near the laborers who were working on the drains in the drive leading to the soccer stadium and the high buildings of Restelo, as the Cape Verdeans' tractors crossed paths with the carts carrying the tombs of princesses and piles of arabesques for altars. Passing by a plaque that identified the unfinished building and said JERONYMITES, we came upon the Tower in the background in the middle of the river, surrounded by Iraqi tankers, defending the nation from Castilian invasions, and, closer by, sitting on the frilly waves by the shore, waiting for the colonists, held fast to the sludge of the water by roots of iron, with admirals in lace cuffs leaning on the rail of the bridge and seamen up on the masts preparing the sails for the open sea that smelled of nightmare and gardenias, among rowboats and a swirl of canoes, we found the ship of the discoveries waiting.

His father died of scurvy before they reached Cape Bojador, when the waters by the bow were as calm as the dust in a library, and they rotted away for a month eating chestnuts and salted meat until the wind shook the hull and knocked against one another the chandelier prisms that were sailors from an abortive mutiny hanged from the rigging, plucked clean by seagulls and Atlantic kites. After seven bloody uprisings, eleven attacks by wandering whales, countless masses, and a tempest just like the sighs God gives in his stony insomnia, a lookout bellowed land, on the bridge astern the skipper grabbed his telescope and there was the bay of Loanda, inverted by the refraction of distance, São Paulo fort on its height, fishing trawlers, a navy corvette, ladies having tea under the palm trees, and plantation owners getting their shoes shined as they read newspapers in the pastry shops under the arcades.

And now as the aircraft was landing in Lixbon he was startled by the buildings in Encarnação, the vacant lots where broken pianos and rupestrine carcasses of automobiles were ossifying, and the cemeteries and military posts whose names he didn't know, as if he were arriving at a foreign city that was missing, in order for him to recognize it as his, the clerks and ambulances of eighteen years before. He'd been delayed for a week with the mulatto woman and the child in the waiting room of the airport in Loanda, lying on the floor, rolled up in blankets, gnawed by hunger and the urge to urinate, in a confusion of suitcases, sacks, children sobbing, and smells, hoping for an opening in order to flee from Angola and the machine guns that were singing in the streets every day, brandished by blacks in camouflage, drunk from cups of aftershave and authority. An official who leafed through papers and leaped over the reclining bodies would dribble out a name every hour or so, and behind the glass windows militiamen of UNITA, with horsehair bracelets and plumed lances, led by American and Chinese advisers, kept watch over us under the fluorescent tubes on the ceiling.

Instead of the labyrinthine market of the day of their departure that came after the maniacal countesses' palaces and the bars with lugubrious shadows and anemic foreigners, instead of the banks of the Tagus where they were building the monastery and stonecutters chipped limestone with great mallet blows, instead of wagons with their oxen and mules and architects bellowing threnodies like the gabble of Galician restaurant workers at their helpers, instead of women selling eggs and chickens and grilled porgies and miniatures of Algarve chimneys and tin knickknacks, instead of the teardrop clarity of the onions on wooden trays, the burning occult powers of Gypsy women who excited autumnal virgins with promises of the love of a viceroy, instead of tourist vans with blue windshields and the caravels and the Turkish freighters under the bridge, they shooed me into a miserable cement building with panels that listed domestic and international flights, with their colored ampules pulsating beside the duty-free whiskey shop. A vending machine for chocolates and cigarettes was shivering with fever in a corner, vomiting candy after a complicated digestion of coins, and the passengers from the plane were lining up in single file as in the crowded grocery stores, bakeries, and butcher shops of Loanda, in search of the rice, bread, and meat that was no longer there, only dust and rinds and fat and a clerk whom the broom hadn't swept away, shaking his head behind the counter, pointing to the empty cases. And he remembered the frightening nightfalls of the last days in Angola, the black urchins who attacked offices and apartments downtown, the building fronts gaping with bullet holes, and the worthy ladies of the Marçal district with no customers, offering their orphaned-mermaid hips to no one in alleys where jeep headlights looked like the lanterns on the caboose of a train.

Those who returned with him, clergymen, Genoese astrologers, Jewish merchants, governesses, slave smugglers, poor whites from the Prenda district, the Cuca district, clinging to burlap bundles, suitcases tied with cords, wicker baskets, broken toys, formed a serpentine line of lamentations and misery up to the airport, pushing their baggage along with their feet (on the walkway reserved for passengers in transit, Icelanders, tall and shaggy like river birds, passed by) toward a desk where sitting on a stool was the king's official chronicler who asked him his name (Pedro Álvares *what?*), checked him on a typed list full of corrections and X marks in pencil, took off his reading glasses to get a better look at him, leaning to one side on his Formica roost, ran his thumb idly over his mustache, and suddenly asked Do you have family in Portugal? and I said No, sir, quickly, without thinking, because my old lady had died of jaundice six years before and I almost can't remember or never remember the uncles and aunts who stayed here, I don't know whether they were still in Coruche and if they were, where they live, who they're living with, how many children they've got, if they're even still alive. I still have a picture in my head of the vague figure of a cousin arriving on leave in his recruit's uniform, treading down the lettuce in the garden with his cruel boots, but the house, for example, what can you do? has disappeared for me, except the mirror in the vestibule bought at the Almeirim fair in the midst of the wailing of suckling pigs and the drums of acrobats, which deformed faces and twisted movements into dim waves, giving back to everyone his secret and genuine face, the one that only the solitude of sleep or the abandon of love will finally reveal. I remember the winters with plantings in lead pots and pans on the floor in order to receive the rain that dribbled down through the cracks in the roof, and, further back in time, my father's godmother mending socks and long underwear beneath the sterile cherry tree in the rear, which was lifting one of the legs of the laundry basin with the bicep force of its roots. And that remote memory suddenly brought to his nose the smell of cow manure from recent months, ever since the telephone call announcing the independence of Angola decreed by His Majesty, during the embers of an uprising, when the court was meeting in Lixbon, the smell of sweat, diarrhea, fear, when, in panic, we pushed closets up against the windows because at any moment a slipper will squash down the carpet, laughing, at any moment the MPLA will start shooting wildly and the backs of heads will burst like figs into a paste of white meat and red seeds, what would the Prince think, if he were alive, there at the school in Sagres, unrolling maps and consulting the stars at the windows by the sea, while his captains chased Danish girls on the beaches of Albufeira and Gil Eanes presented himself in Lagos, dripping like an exhausted bridegroom, with a bouquet of withered flowers in his hand. He said Not a trace, and he thought Of course not, because in eighteen years in Africa I never received a letter, a postcard, a ham, not even a photograph. I'll almost bet that they all died centuries ago, buried under slabs in churches with their names in Latin obliterated by the soles of novice nuns, comfortable in the pearl-colored lining of their coffins, dressed in checkered jackets, lilac shawls, white blouses, with crossed hands and jagged jaws like the recumbent statues in chapel crypts. My family with their jaws tied and silver coins on the eyes that stared at me with disapproval, This is the one who went to Loanda to live surrounded by blacks instead of taking advantage of a tobacco shop in Venezuela or a travel agency in Germany, this is the one who opened up a butcher shop in the slums, selling chops to niggers, had a son by a mulatto woman, lived in a prefabricated hut in Cuca, who didn't

even own a car, a boat, on Sundays would sprawl out in the parlor
in his drawers listening to soccer games and eating the shit of a
native's life, the chronicler made assiduous Gothic notes in front
of my name, wiggling his wise ears as if he shared the disdain or
the displeasure of my aunts and uncles, and the deacon who was
his acolyte, with the crown of hair and chubby cheeks of a ceramic Saint Anthony, repeated No relatives, no brother-in-law,
no distant relation?, while he filled out forms, multiplied figures on a pocket calculator, handed me a paper to sign, Here,
he poured a drop of wax at the bottom of the page and gave it
to the other one to seal the nodule of steaming blood with his
crested ring. The mulatto woman, in plastic sandals and a ker-
chief tied around her head, who before living with me had waited
on tables in a restaurant in Ilha, sank into a poster of oriental
vacations that showed a couple with wreaths around their necks
taking their ease in a marine sunset with mugs of beer. Nobody,
I said, just the bedroom furniture that should arrive on the next
galleon if it didn't disappear on the docks with all this business
of thievery, democracy, and socialism, and I was proud of the
bed tables with porcelain knobs, the cupboard with three doors
for bottles, crystal, and wine- and water glasses, along with the
bureau that had a sumptuous marble top on which the veins that
branch out lightly on the eyelids of small children were engraved,
at the same time that, with the pomp of awarding a diploma
magna cum laude, the clerk gave me an illegible notice, You've
got a week in which to appear at the office there, *agora veja là*.
Behind me a plebeian on crutches was protesting the delays of
bureaucracy, When I get out of here I'm going to complain to
the newspapers, and I stopped listening to him because I remembered Coruche again and my father's godmother limping about

the house, with the clothes basket *das molas* in her hands, out of focus in the trellis with the grapevines. As for room and board, the clerk explained, indifferent to the man on crutches, without even looking at or worrying in the least about the mulatto woman and the boy who was wrapped around my legs, mouth open in a spiral of anxiety, we've arranged a place for you at the Apostle of the Indies Boarding House on the Largo de Santa Bárbara, take a bus and ask for Mr. Francisco Xavier, next. A heavy, timid redhead, stammering what he wanted, elbowed me out of the way to get close to the desk and we were all alone and abandoned in a city that I knew and didn't know and which had the sweet smell of the wild boars that mountain hunters set their dogs on in the summertime, pursuing them through the squares and alleys of Linda-a-Velha or Bucelas, while Dutch merchants and captains from the Malaccan seas disappeared into taxis at the airport on their way downtown and the ebb-tide stench of its alleys, and the three of us there outside, on the sidewalk, *à torreira,* waiting for the little tables from Angola as if the caravels would cross through the avenues and deposit at our feet a crate mildewed with sandbar sludge, chewed soft by the gums of waves, broken up by opposing currents and the sharpness of reefs, bearded with mussels and oceanic oysters, with the remains of a mattress and a knob inside.

Once upon a time there was a man named Luís who was missing his left eye and who remained on the Alcântara docks for three or four weeks at least, sitting on top of his father's coffin, waiting for the rest of his goods to arrive on the next ship. He'd given the stevedores, a drunken Portuguese sergeant, and the customs officials the deed to his house and all the money he had, he'd seen them hoist the refrigerator, stove, and ancient Chevrolet with a ranting motor on board a ship that was already being made ready, but he refused to leave the casket in spite of the orders of a chubby major (You can't be dreaming of taking that crap with you), a coffin with carved handles and a crucifix on the lid, dragged tilting along to the amazement of the commandant, who forgot about his vernier and lifted his head, dizzy with calculations, to look at him at the moment the man called Luís was disappearing below and was stowing the dead man under his bunk, the way the other passengers did with their baskets and suitcases. Then he stretched out on the blanket, put his hands behind his neck, and amused himself by following the meticulous crochet work of the spiders and the zeal of the mice on the ceiling beams covered with crabs and barnacles, dreaming about the nocturnal arms of absent black women. At the second lunch he met a retired cardsharp and a one-handed Spaniard who'd been selling lottery tickets in Mozambique named Don Miguel de Cervantes Saavedra, a former soldier, always writing on the pages torn out of a ledger and discarded scraps of paper a novel entitled, no one knew why, *Quixote,* when everybody knew that Quixote is the nickname of a steeplechase horse, and at the end of the afternoon they pulled out the coffin and played some fine blackjack on the varnished cover, avoiding touching the crucifix, because it's risky in cards and can affect your hand, and lifting up their buckled shoes whenever the listing of the ship spilled the vomit of their neighbors in their direction; it had reached a depth of six inches and obliged them, sopping their stockings, to hold on to the handles so the corpse wouldn't get away from them, adrift in a soup where *lavagantes* fluttered, carrying off the jacks and aces of the winning hand.

The man named Luís had been living with his father in Cazenga when a patrol fired on the old man, and that was how his domino-playing friends brought him to him, wrapped in torn sheets with just a lock of sandy hair sticking out; they laid him on the dining room table on top of the plates and silverware, and went off arguing about a double six; he went down the alley to the funeral parlor that a grenade had blown up, went in through the glass shards of the show window, and picked out a casket from among the many left over in the store, because bodies were decomposing on squares and in the streets without anybody's being concerned about them except stray dogs and ragpickers. He rolled the decedent inside it, forgetting to unwrap the sheet around him, to kiss him, to dress him in his wedding suit, or to trim his nails, tightened the screws on the casket, and the very next morning put it onto a wheelbarrow along with a change of clothing and a lunch pail of potatoes and headed for the docks with the idea of embarking for the realme. As soon as the vomit reached a foot in height, he moored the coffin to the leg of the bunk with the pack thread from the Christmas turkeys, so he could sleep even if he sensed his father floating weightlessly inside his sleep, calling to him through the chinks in the walnut wood with the agitated voice of the dead. When they docked in Lixbon, the one-handed man and the retiree helped him put the coffin, which was missing a few handles and pieces of the mourning ribbon, on the edge of the dock, and the retiree took the cards out of his pocket for one last game underneath the bridal moans of the derricks, the borborygmy of the corvettes, and the albatrosses that were conspiring up above, intrigued by the old man's vinegar smell. After the thirteenth round the lottery man stood up, Buenas noches, gentlemen, I've got to get to Spain and finish my book, I can only read proof with the Gypsy sun of Madrid at the head of my bed, I promise to mail autographed copies to both of you, and they noticed then with surprise that people and baggage had disappeared from the docks: all that was left was darkness, a tortured deserter in a kind of chair for the edification of people and food for crows, and a lighted lamp in a lifeguard station or maritime office, one of those that the ministry of fisheries or the Prince Navigator and the Judiciary Police had set up down the shore to keep watch at the same time on hashish smuggling and on the maneuvers of Flemish buccaneers. The tonality of the waves against the stones had changed, transparent and soft now, like the sound of your eyes. The retiree won the one hundred forty-ninth implacable game when the markings on the cards could no longer be made out and they had to guess the value of the face by a deceptive echo in their souls, after which he gathered up the deck, said good-bye, and went off, lamenting, so as not to be upset, that with partners like that, who didn't even know the figures on the cards, what pleasure was there in winning a hand? The man named Luís sat for ages watching the card player going off with the prudent little steps of those who are on subtly familiar terms with chance until he disappeared, gray against the gray sky, beyond a row of bushes parallel to a railroad track and was lost in the illuminated disorder of the city. Then he sat down on the coffin with the water at his feet, unable to make it out except for the panting of the river as it went away and came back, and where the sewers of Lixbon poured out along with pastoral sonnets by the poet Francisco Rodrigues Lobo, a suicide in the Tagus fished up in a net like a mustachioed shad. The gulls and kites roosted on the almost finished cornices of the Jeronymites, to which the army had transferred the gloriously modest little flame of the unknown soldier, a champion flung into the French mud and German gases of the First World War, giving way to bats the size of partridges, which slept during the day in the peace of the cloister's archways that had a small pool in the center destined for the child siren that Bartholomeu Dias had promised the king on his next voyage, as soon as the song of a conch shell rose up early in the morning from the reefs and dazzled the sailors. Maneuvering locomotives cut off the man named Luís from the buildings along the shore, obliquely placed on the pavement like the ships in the moss of the Tagus during the siege of the city. A corporal of the customs guard, with a musket, dressed in the stripes of the Swiss who protect the pope, passed him by once or twice, smoking, and the Morse code of the tip of his cigarette answered the flashlight message of the smugglers directing the small naval fleet of false Moroccan trawlers loaded to the gunwales with Italian liquor and opium poppies. It smelled of heat and garbage and from time to time leftover newspapers raised up a breeze of recent events from the sidewalk. I urinated in the shadow of a fruit truck and while I was unbuttoning my fly and the air was tinged with the fragrance of peaches, I remembered Loanda at six in the afternoon, at the hour when the boats were going out to fish, getting smaller as they smoked between the trunks of palm trees. I urinated thinking about the deaf-mute's watch store, Charlie Chaplin eyes surrounded by hundreds of furious cuckoos as he repaired microscopic springs, forty feet from where I worked, thinking about Don Miguel de Cervantes Saavedra, who would sometimes declaim strange episodes of Dulcineas and windmills for us and would add, all excited, touching the pencil in his jacket, I'm going to put that in my book, thinking about the retired cardsharp, who would plug the cracks in the coffin with strips of cloth and candle wax and sit beside me on the bunk showing me old photographs pasted in a school notebook, This is me on a rocking horse at the age of four, The third from the left is me in the army in Tancos, This was taken of me by my brother Paulo when I discovered the sea route to India, Here, this is a funny one, look, I'm with my fellow workers in the label section of the brewery, as a token they gave me a pen with a gold tip and a framed certificate with a plaque underneath and everybody's signature, What a shame you don't work here anymore, Gama, the retiree who went on and on with endless episodes of his youth as a shoemaker in Vila Franca, land whose redness the Tagus sometimes displayed, sometimes hid, depending on the floods, leaving behind as it withdrew the bloated bellies of oxen and stuffed saxophones on the bandstand. The cousin who ran the shoe business had written him in Africa offering him a room and a partnership in the store, and I, who didn't know anyone in Portugal, memorized the address in order to visit him during Easter with a bag of muffins and an

American deck of cards with naked women on the backs. I finished urinating just as a locomotive started up, mingling its call with the call of the ships, and I went back to the docks, not knowing what to do with the hindrance of the coffin, to which the one-handed lottery man, with the absurd impulse of an artist, had promised a poem, I'll get down from my horse in Madrid, shut myself up in my house, and write it in a matter of seconds, it's no effort at all, a cinch, I'll copy everything onto onion-skin paper and it will be here in a month at most. I scratched the herpes incrustations on my ear, spat into the invisible water in hopes of an idea, but where in hell could I bury my father since I didn't even have the money for a funeral service? If you weren't a complete fool, the retiree explained to me, maneuvering checkers, in one of his rare moments of compassion and harsh friendship, you would have left the deceased behind on the table where they laid him with his hand and its long nails almost grabbing the cruet, because those people go crazy for oil, like owls, who suck it up in food warehouses flapping their wings, but I was bothered by the idea of his rotting away all alone in Africa with calendulas in the hairs of his nose, surrounded by salamanders and scorpions. With the seventh spit dawn broke: a clay light revealed the cranes, the outlines of the ships from Ceylon, the flames from the steel mill in the distance, and the skeleton of the tortured man on his gibbet altar. The kites and crows returned, the customs guard corporal disappeared. Some fishermen in printed shirts set themselves up ten or twenty yards from the coffin, each with his creel and his pole, but after a few hours of not catching anything they threw their gear into a gas company truck and took off in the same direction more or less as Mr. Gama and the Spaniard, the loose canvas on top shaking as they went over the railroad tracks, and after they left night returned: the lights went on, the lamps on canoes swayed, the unfinished mass of the Jeronymites, watched over by yeomen with halberds, took on an unforeseen grandeur. The corporal from the night before peeped out of his booth of roofing tiles, and whenever he approached the buckles of his leggings sparkled and his features were reduced to inexpressive wooden lumps. The bats sniffing around bulbs in search of the tropical moths that had arrived with the slaves from Guinea mistakenly dove into the purple reflections on the faint waves of the Tagus. Automobiles, with their headlights on dim, in which lovers rolled around, aimed their sullen grillwork at the ground. The smell from the coffin had gradually become as unbearable as that of the deserter on his stump, with birds perched on the crest of his spine and what was left of his shoulders and buttocks, so I thought As soon as the refrigerator and stove arrive, I'm going to sell them to some Gypsy and buy the old man a Jesus a yard and a half tall, with carving and decorations, since, after a certain age, we spend our lives imagining, perfecting, polishing the macabre theatrics of our own funeral rites, the sexton, the family, the announcements in the newspaper, the interest of neighbors, how many wreaths and how many quarts of tears. I thought: I haven't even got enough to pay people to cry. I thought: I haven't even got enough to buy dark glasses and a great big emigrant's good-bye handkerchief to pretend I'm crying. I thought: Or to hire any beggars who exaggerate their hunger on the steps of churches to pose as relatives, and at that moment the corporal, after trying in vain to give a quick silken kick to a cat, came over diagonally, like a lobster, shifting the sling of his weapon from one shoulder to the other.

"What's that there?" he asked.

Only then did I realize that beyond the locusts and grass-hoppers in the shadows, whose trill is like the buzzing of the spangles of insomnia, beyond the mollusks in the shrouds and the harp of the rigging and its single ceaselessly repeated note, a cricket was chirping: not in the night, mind you; on a small anchored boat, one of those flatboats for hunters of sludge and sick shellfish with a crew of men with their pantlegs rolled up carrying shrimp nets and buckets. From time to time a small fin would sparkle with a leap out of the water and evaporate again. The houses, duplicated, with their legs in the air, rose and fell toward Lixbon, adorned with carnations in the boxes on their balconies. The corporal touched the casket with the tip of his boot, assessing it:

"Does this shit belong to you?"

At dawn, when locomotives call, even from far away, they give the impression that they're so close you could hug them against your chest. Other sounds too. And the silence. And the smells. And the voices that whisper miles away: everything close by, clear, transparent and fragile, made of glass. Including the bridge crossing the Tagus and the fireflies of the trucks floating on its tray.

"I'm waiting for the packet so I can take it away from here," I said. "I've got my dead father wrapped in a sheet in there."

In Africa, strewn with stone markers, the remains of caravels, and the armor of dead conquerors, screech owls plant themselves in the middle of clearings and let the cars run over them, owls with yellow eyes like the fins in the water and the fireflies of the trucks: we would see them too late, blow the horn, and a swirl of ash-gray feathers, more like hairs than feathers, would strike the windshield and die behind us, getting lost in the fields of sunflowers where wild asses trotted ceaselessly. In Africa, unlike here, my nose would touch the smells and be happy, legs knew the places to walk, hands learned objects easily, you breathed an air cleaner than church cloth, until the civil war took a shot at the old man, shut me up with the retiree and the one-handed man with the windmills in the hold of a ship, and the smells and sounds in the dark became foreign to me because I don't know this city, because I don't know these alleys and their illusory shadows, because I can only make out the port and the trawlers, present by day and absent by night, not to mention the crows and gulls, excited by the dead man's dew, pecking at the crucifix in search of the hidden rotting meat in the varnished tomb.

"A corpse?" The corporal was mistrustful. "A corpse or American tobacco, my friend? Gitanes, Marlboros, anisette, French perfume, vermouth, a dozen Japanese transistor radios? Are you trying to convince me that you've got a corpse in there?"

He flung away his cigarette butt and the little light wandered off into the night and was extinguished in the Tagus. The grade crossing began to ring with the bewildered fury of alarm clocks and the windows of the ten o'clock express went by, one after the other, behind the shrubbery, with flashing squares, carrying with it the workers on the Jeronymites to their neighborhoods on the outskirts without electricity or running water, with drunkards and bitches in heat raving on the corners. A pair of guards, summoned by the corporal's whistle, carried the coffin into the tiled office with broken-down desks up against the wall, ancient metal file cases and service orders and reports of missing ships pinned to a cork board to the left of the framed photograph of the president of the republic, who was gazing into eternity with the visionary stupidity of heroes. The guards, squatting down, loosened the screws, crumbled the coat of stearin that encircled the coffin, used jackknives to unplug the stuffing in breaks in the lining; an ammonia wind rose up out of the casket and the president's mouth in the portrait twisted with the grimace of a toothache, with which he had been present for many years over school blackboards.

"As soon as the packet arrives with my things," I guaranteed, "I swear I'll pay for a tombstone, the way it should be."

Near the lamp, more naked without his cap than if he were undressed, the corporal, cleaning his nails with a matchstick, looked like a low-tide sludge fisherman, although with leggings and a cartridge belt around his waist in order to assassinate the eels in the river. Or the bats. Or the trains. Or the Tower for fighting the Castilians. Or the father who'd swallowed his lead in Loanda and was slowly turning into a quagmire of guts.

"God damn it," one of the guards said, nauseous, covering his nose with his drill sleeve. "You just show me that little old Japanese radio, my fine corporal."

A locomotive sped past the life-saving post, knocking over files and chairs, and now the three of them were looking at me, hiding behind a corner of the sheet, with the surprise of virgins, while I took a step with a small humble smile of pardon:

"If you gentlemen would nail up the coffin I'd be thankful: the fact is I haven't got any place to sit until the boat comes."

The Apostle of the Indies Boarding House wasn't located on the Largo de Santa Bárbara as the official chronicler had assured them, but on the slope of some terrain hidden behind buildings between the Italian embassy and the Military Academy. It was a tumbledown house in the midst of tumbledown houses in front of which a group of vagrants were sitting on pieces of canvas and carrying on a shouted conversation around a sick goat. He asked about the address from a halfbreed with shifty eyes, from boys poking through garbage with sticks, and from an alcoholic survivor of distant seas hugging a rusty anchor, and they stumbled around beams from scaffolding, whitewashed walls, twisted chunks of concrete, the remains of a wall and stairs of apartments with nobody in them, where navigational lights slip by across the intervals of the windows at night. A flock of doves on a projection of tiled roof was startled, fanned out, and disappeared into a sky of chimneys. Below, on the Rua de Arroios, with work on the sewers and a Caterpillar tractor blocking traffic, were decrepit millinery shops, whore bars, and whimsical little food stores swarming with workmen with cane-wick candles lighted in the sconces of their hands. A rat damp with brilliantine fled out of a drain, ran along some silted steps, and stole into a pile of rubble. The beggars watched him from a distance, in silence, under a piece of awning, and at that moment he saw the letters APOSTLE OF THE INDIES BOARDING HOUSE painted in yellow beside an open door or what had once been a door and was nothing but a kind of broken-down gate now. A girl wearing men's shoes was emptying a box into a hole full of rinds, insecticide packages, compass faces, and empty syrup bottles. Mr. Francisco Xavier, a fat East Indian in sandals, received him in the ship's cabin of a vestibule, surrounded by a dozen little Indians, all looking like him, also fat and wearing sandals, of various sizes, like the keys on a xylophone. The cabin smelled of insomnia and feet, it smelled of the manure of a poor man's corral, and the migratory movement of the clouds could be seen through the gaps in the plaster. As if there'd been a war here too, Pedro Álvares Cabral thought, as if mortar fire had destroyed the buildings.

"I'm from Mozambique," Mr. Francisco Xavier explained in a heathen-softened accent as he took the landing papers stamped with the clerk's insignia. And he imagined the Goan, an extinguished cigar in the saliva of his jaws, adoring creatures with eight legs in the jungle or fobbing off taffeta cuts from square to square, preceded by the persuasive volume of his belly. Outside one could hear the vagrants arguing in shrill voices and the puffy-necked doves returning to their roosts, and, bending over, I caught a glimpse of the goat shivering in the midst of the rocks and the deserted buildings that were slowly disappearing into the night around me.

"Didn't they tell you," Mr. Francisco Xavier was surprised, "that you have to put down a deposit of five *contos*?"

The girl with the box came back talking to herself and disappeared into the opening of a stairway: the unlaced shoes were catching on the edge of the steps. Whispering and weeping spread out all through the shadows of the boardinghouse. Some bird or other was giving a strangled whistle from a hole in the mortar in a corner.

"In Beira I owned three movie houses and a mansion with a swimming pool," Mr. Francisco Xavier said, displaying the empty arms of a dethroned despot. "Three movie houses and a mansion across from the caravels in the harbor, not to mention the servants, of course, and if anyone had told me I'd be running this hole in order to make a living I would have laughed all afternoon at the least. The unpaid bills the guests stick me with are enough to drive you crazy. Speaking of unpaid bills, boy, have you got the five *contos* or haven't you? Three movie houses, damn it. And just sign this little receipt for me to show I got that amount from you, it's the way we do things at the Apostle of the Indies. Honesty on one side, honesty on the other."

The mulatto woman, ready to collapse, dragged in the suitcases and bags. It must have been eight o'clock in spite of the tomblike silence of the clocks waiting for people to open the awnings on the cabarets on Santa Bárbara, and characters in gold braid, dressed like carnival captains, were directing a complicated traffic of customers and whores. The doves were restless on the broken-down windowsills and he thought that Lixbon without Chinese restaurants was the ugliest city on the face of the earth. He thought, looking at a wasps' nest in a plaster wall, Where am I going to get ahold of five *contos* to keep the fat man quiet, and at that instant there was a squeal from out of the darkness, Hey, Xavier, the Indian told us Take it easy, I'll be right back and he took off with his sandals slapping, followed by the xylophone of children in the direction of the storerooms, landings, rooms, caves, and tunnels of the boardinghouse.

So they remained waiting in the vestibule, facing the squeaking of the *tojo* bush and the August crickets, the mulatto woman

and the boy completely silent, hunched and quiet in the growing darkness, measuring everything, checking out everything,
examining everything, the aimless centipedes, the dead beetles,
the toneless lizards on the projections of the roof, the night and
the milky way of lampposts on Martim Moniz that no finger
untwisted, and me, a white man from Coruche without any in-
stincts or mystery, too far removed from the chestnut trees of
his childhood, thinking about the money for the Indian and how
to steal it, hearing steps and rustling and the dragging of trunks,
remembering my grandfather probing the three o'clock sun with
his cane until the voice of Mr. Francisco Xavier proclaimed as
his frowsy sandals grew closer again I've arranged for a room for
you with eight other families from Angola, what a piece of luck
for you, devilishly lucky, all the same country, all together, all
buddies, all fun, how about those five little *contos,* eh, chum?

This time he didn't have the long procession of kids bringing
up the rear, but a a tiny, barefoot old woman, hair in a bun and
parted in the middle with a red spot on her forehead, a playing-
card heart between the chapel arches of her graying eyebrows,
and in her eyes there was the reflection of pools of crocodiles,
the silhouettes of pirates, and the ships of Dom João de Castro
under a catastrophe sky riding at anchor in the jaundiced sea of
Diu. A centenary old woman brought from Malabar or Timor
along with the first peppers, the mistress of bearded discoverers
with thick, barrel coughs, who was conversing with Mr. Francisco Xavier in the colorful language of the wooden idols that
sleep under immense trees in their copper pagodas, the ancient
sweetheart of sailors, who, undaunted, had witnessed fierce
boardings, scurvy's ulcerations, fumigation with balms, and the
melancholy of viceroys leaning over balconies watching the sun-

set swallows. She wasn't much interested in the little one or me, who were occupied in measuring the density of the night by the speed of owls, but she went forward and stepped back several times in the direction of the mulatto woman, observing her face, body, legs, and I felt that I was on the waterfront or in the market in Cascais on a morning full of shouts, parrots, anger, haggling, witnessing the landing of slaves with rooster feathers at the backs of their necks, through hatchways on the frigates. The fat man pressed a hand switch and a sudden brightness revealed the decorated courtyard where rubbish was swimming, the loose planks from the deck of a command bridge, the plaster in pieces, the wounds, stains, and scars of the stucco. The vagrants were warming themselves for sleep on the vacant lot, gathering together newspapers against the summer dew. Stray dogs and unfrocked archbishops with miters of glass strips on their heads fluttered like stumbling angels close to the door. The girl with the box came out into the night to smoke, disguised as a doll from a neighborhood bazaar, with straw cheeks and neck tied with a leprous stole. Mr. Francisco Xavier, spread over a corner of the counter, was arduously copying our names in a ruled notebook with the Gothic calligraphy of newspaper headlines.

A watchdog howled fifty yards away from us and then a second one, farther on, answered from the gasoline station with a painful lament, his throat amplified by the cement shell of the garage with other voices inside there, of drivers, mail deliverers, upholsterers, the last mechanic, soaping himself up at a spigot whose water spread out, shining along the cracks in the floor: I know what it's like from having worked as an apprentice years ago in a repair shop in Sá da Bandeira in the midst of fumes of oil, leather, and oakum, watching electricians repairing batteries on greasy workbenches full of trash and amp meters under the curdled milk of the fluorescent lights. I quit because the foreman caught me with my finger in the jacket of the body man looking for a few innocent pennies for a pack of cigarettes and he threw me out, up the ramp into the rainy street, giving me a whack. The Indian, drawn away by the faith of the gospels from his smiling idols and monstrous thunderstorms, came over from behind the counter with the flab of his belly swaying over his belt:

"Haven't you got the dough, young fellow?"

The rats, who were conspiring in the space above the ceiling, broke off a piece of plaster from up there and the old woman, openmouthed, leaped like a crippled toad, gripped the mulatto woman with the pincers of her claws, and dragged her into the tunnels of the Apostle of the Indies, where a child was shrieking in the parlor decorated with seventeenth-century tiles from the first floor representing hunting scenes or the miracles of virgins. And I got to thinking as to whether the beggars' goat slept standing up, its knees trembling in the thistles in the vacant lot.

"You haven't got even one miserable cent left, confess to the boss, now," Mr. Francisco Xavier grew merry, clapping me happily on the back while up from the riverbank the wind carried the smell of heroic oilcloth from the hydroplane without propellers exposed beyond Beato on the pontoons used by Sunday fishermen, with the passengers still sitting in their seats as could be glimpsed through the sweat of the portholes.

"Don't pay it any mind, because in my case it was three first-run movie houses with four hundred seats each," Mr. Francisco Xavier consoled him. "At carnival time I would organize dances in the lobby, masquerade contests, free drinks, there were gas balloons for the urchins, the kind that on the second day can't decide between the ceiling and the floor, a group came from Nampula that specialized in mambos, a barrel of dough that all went up in smoke."

The streetlights in Arroios, the streetlights in Paço da Rainha were twinkling at the foot of the hill like the torches of Dom Pedro I's nighttime revelry, and my son, still glued to my sleeve, still clutching my knees, still hooked on to my waist, was staring at me with intense, adult, serious eyes, which, ever since his birth in an army hospital, had never caught sight of the moonlight of any childhood: a microscopic little man who didn't look at all like me or anybody in my family, a gnome coming directly from remote black grandparents in the jungles of Carmona sitting on mats by the entrance to straw huts with a calabash pipe in their hands. I rubbed against the doorjamb, sniffing, but this Lixbon night doesn't smell of coffee groves, of the boss's house with columns in the virgin grass, of the outline of São Paulo fort, of the broad and deep breathing of the earth: it smells of butane, of the smoke of wealth, of the stink of centuries gone by, of friars' mules, and of the feces of a sick goat in a lumpy vacant lot. The bulb in the vestibule blinked, confusing the gnats. The traffic lights on the Avenida Almirante Reis were drawing the vehicles toward the smugglers' square of Martim Moniz and the guitars of its beggars who repeat ad nauseam the complaints of homeless caulkers of the sea. Mr. Francisco Xavier called to me from the counter, closing the book with ecclesiastical solemnity, and I caught sight of the mulatto woman dressed like a puppet or a circus clown, like the girl in men's shoes, her kinky hair done up in a bun with bows, silver fingernails, lipstick, green eyelids, and a question mark of surprise on her knitted brow. The old woman, needle in hand, was hurriedly arranging the lamé pleats around her thighs.

"Your wife will work down there in a bar until the small matter of the room rent is paid," the Indian decided, vigorously scratching his groin. "If things go well for us, boy, in no time it'll be better than having three movie houses in Lourenço Marques."

There's nothing to know about me: I drag the wicker rocking chair from the center of the vestibule from where the door can be seen and the flooring of the second story creaks less, I turn out the light and sit waiting, breathing heavily in the darkness, for them to return from the clubs on Arroios or from the trees in the Campo de Santana, exhausted, hair straggly, shoes in hand, lipstick smeared from customers' kisses, followed at a distance by the barking of dogs, the horns of resentful cars, and the fife of the wind in the weeds and ruined buildings. After dinner I relax for a while, chewing my cigar with my eyes open in the night, and after two following the patrol car as it lights up the broken blinds and disappears into the Italian embassy, I get up slowly so as not to wake up my mother and my children who sleep in the same bed as I, go down the steps cupping my belly in the palms of my hands, and sit down to watch the traffic lights and signs on Estefânia, names with fused letters, and chunks of tiled roof that the tomato-colored moon reveals and sharpens, thinking about the three movie houses I never had, only a large room with bedbugs in the damned Pakistani quarter, a sweaty den where you couldn't breathe from the smell of curry, with cowboys galloping a little behind the unsynchronized sound of their horses' hooves on the sheet that served as a screen. Thinking about Africa, beloved brothers, and the mansion with the swimming pool that was nothing but a basin for washing clothes with a depth of rainwater rotting inside in the grass beside the trailer we lived in, bought from the bankrupt circus that deposited its giraffes and lions with the pawnbrokers in the city, worn-out beasts with overcoat elbows stretched out in shop windows among bracelets and alarm clocks, or poor clowns in showcases laughing at us with their enormous melancholy guffaws.

So I listen to the sound of the rocking chair and the varied, strange, multiple, tiny sounds in the house, the beetles' little steps in the silence, the agitation of the silverfish, the snoring of the guests, I listen to morning arriving, still dark, in the stirring of the birds in holes roundabout, while I wait for the women to climb up the hill from the wild vodka discotheques in the Bairro das Colónias and on Luciano Cordeiro, who come into the boarding house all dopey from cheap wine, who pass by without even noticing me, reaching out my arm for the last one, the most drunken and drowsy and unwary of them all, flattening her up against the lumps on the counter, lifting up the sequins of her skirt and furrowing her thighs, forcibly, with the energy of a plow, while the chair rocks on the floor, back and forth with its straw seat, until my jerking stops at the same time as the sighs from the wood, she smooths her dress with a rustle of paper carnations that mingle with the sound of the wings of the doves, and I leave, adjusting my fly, to chase away the snout of the first stray dog that comes out of the night to spy from the doorway on the Boarding House sepulcher, on the sleeping mummies of the guests.

No movie houses and no swimming pool: just a shack falling apart among the pieces of hut that encircle the ancient city of slave merchants, and my wife, thirty-one years and seven months younger than I, swapped with my chum for an airplane ticket to Lixbon: You keep her and the furniture and just give me the little piece of paper for the flight. My chum, squatting on the rug like a buoy, resting his blowhole, took measure of the girl, hesitant, and then he stared at me, mistrustful: With so many people going off now there must be a wild lot of business in Europe. And he ended up saying he had to consult for three days with a niece who read cards and predicted eclipses, and that in the meantime, in order to weigh the value of the transaction, he would take my wife for testing purposes, because How do I know if she can sew, how do I know if she can cook. She still hasn't grown up and she hasn't got any illnesses, I reassured him, I had a devil of a time getting her to obey, but she does everything you tell her to, she irons clothes, knows Indian recipes, can help you sell native idols, where *aos oitenta* will you find a chippy like that?

After three days (it was raining even though it wasn't hot thereabouts, only the taciturn ecstasy of the narcissuses and the usual five hundred million mosquitoes biting me on the ears) I pounded on the zinc door early in the morning after dragging my sandals two hundred yards along the alley: thumping on the corrugated metal for at least half an hour until my chum shouted Who's there? from the swampy mist of his sleep. Through the openings between the metal sheets you could sense the darkness inside, full of the bronchitis of hens and sleeping people crushed in by the weight of the furniture. I peeped It's me just as the rain grew harder and the sky smelled of brimstone and dried garlic and the boulders of the first thunderclaps exploded, rolling over the straw roofs. Open the door for your husband, my chum commanded, his voice growing in the siphon of the wind, and after a while the crossbeam ran through the warped slot, the girl appeared, barefoot, with a pot in her hand, and there was the usual almost complete lack of furniture gathering flot-sam in the corners, wire frames with colored pictures of actresses in bathing suits, the gewgaws by Kaffir craftsmen that he foisted off on people from café to café and from terrace to terrace, the ceramic roosters, the broken basin and my chum in bed, sweat-ing the smell of old shoe leather, his eyes hazy from the myopia of fever: I've come down with a rough dose of malaria, I've been dragging around vomiting since yesterday. And my wife, just imagine, the daughter of a white merchant, the daughter of the owner of the only bar for a mile around, helping him with cool compresses on his chest and head, much more submissive and solicitous than at any time with me, even last winter when I twisted around on my mattress for six days trying to pass some kidney stones, cleaning him maternally, him, who could have been her great-grandfather, wiping the drops off his mustache and sideburns, the big whore. Give the man the ticket, Lourdes, my chum said from his bed of pain, and the white woman stuck her hand into a pot, fumbled through the sound of keys, and came over to me with the walk of a mongrel dog that I'd no-ticed on her the first time I'd seen her walking from the corian-der patch in the garden to her father's prefab, tall, blond, strong, a docile mare who went up two galley steps at a time, a great big basket in the crook of her arm, disappearing into the house without looking at me and she left a kind of aquarium gas bub-bling in my bones, a dizziness, mommy, like now, making way for me, wrapped in what from close by looked like a towel, and that way you could see her naked body underneath, her broad breasts, her smooth belly, the reddish froth of her hair. A duck invaded the room and tried to climb up unsuccessfully, always falling, onto a ragged canvas chair with strips of raffia on the armrests. If you've already got the papers for Lixbon, beat it, my chum squeaked from the bedcovers where he was dissolving into the soaked fabric, thinner and more skull-faced than ever, and I thought, without ceasing to admire her, evaluating the muscular serenity of her shoulders and pubis, I want to call off the deal, what the hell, I want to grab her by the hair and take her away with me. Thinking better about it, I said to the sick man, The one who's losing in this swap is me, and my chum sat up in his sheets, furious, with a compress sliding down his cheek, staring at me with his irrevocable tiny red eyes, dim from the affliction of the malaria and the countless years of his age, skeletal, fragile, and unexpectedly enormous in the inconceivable puniness of his limbs. Give your husband what we agreed on and come over here, and my wife placed the ticket on the corner of the table and went over, drawn by that unquavering voice of a haughty sparrow, almost leaning her hip against the man's ear. The duck quacked in panic, with one of its wings caught on the canvas, leaping with an open bill, unable to free itself. There were shoes, broken coffeepots, and mango seeds on the floor, lace panties, ribs of fans, boxes of buttons. You have to show up at the airport tonight, my chum advised, shaken by coughing, have you checked the boarding time yet? And she, the blockhead, fixing the pillows, lighting the broken jets of the stove, making him some herbal tea, moving behind dunes of trash with a conjugal familiarity that revolted me. The duck managed to free itself from the cords of the chair and escaped under the bed with an offended waddle. The rain was dripping on the bedcovers, dripping on my head, dripping on the girl and on the old man and on the duck who were staring at me in unison with the same hostility or indifference, and I caught the plane (it was still raining) just as they were making the last call. This gate over here, please. I walked along under an open canopy in the direction of the steps that the lightning flashes revealed before everything fell back into a sad and listless night. The aircraft ran the length of the strip that was almost without lights and lifted up over the opaque blur of the sea. I mean: you couldn't see anything no matter what except for our own reflections in the windows, but I knew it was the sea, and I remembered how many times, as a child, I'd looked at those waves remembering Goa.

A missionary priest, transported by a lost skiff and whom scurvy and malaria had made as thin as an Abyssinian without a place to hang his hat, had married them fifty-three years before in the Guinea that at the time was limited to a cluster of houses on the estuary of the river, many of them of wood and grass, with children and alligators playing on the same rocks in the same cradles made of sticks around the government house and a not very majestic hermitage. Boa constrictors grew fat in the dampness of ponds and the lady in mourning from whom they'd rented the room spent the day with one shoe on and the other off, a patent-leather boot in the air squashing gnats against the wall. On Sundays, when bodies sought each other and touched in the sheets musty from the heat, the uneven walking of the lady on the ground floor amidst the hundreds of pendulums, each going its own way, and the vengeful explosions of the sole on the brick wall, ended up taking the spirit out of their desire and making them go out into the street, blinded by the light, to sit down on the benches in a small square with dwarf mango trees whose trunks stood out in the damp fog. Or they went down to the docks, drawn by the tattooed curiosity of the natives, witnessing the always identical docking of the immigrants, dark people from Trás-os-Montes or Beira, waxen in the waxy drowsiness of the afternoon, who descended from the deck with the processional slowness of a funeral. In the course of those fifty-three years dozens more chapels had been built and immediately went to ruin, a neighborhood for the workers from the Gongorist sonnet factory and for the unemployed chroniclers who combed cedillas from their beards, and a sewage system perpetually clogged by toad embryos. The mosquito keeper died of bladder trouble and the insects went on to circulate freely in spite of the geckos, the broken-down heater for the kitchen cupboard, the enameled medallion coasters (girls and fauns lunching on a lawn) under the bottles of port. The lower floor was first occupied by a plantation overseer, who did secret business in Siamese twins and tin novelties with the police of the realme, followed by a poet with powdered hair and shoes with buckles and high heels who boasted of having been a friend of the late and glorious Manoel Maria Barbosa Du Bocage, I was the one who witnessed the birth in bars on the Rossio of the most beautifully improvised verses of any time, and later, in wartime now, by officers gnawed away by intestinal fever, who would change faces and insignia of rank every two years and come back out of the jungle with a fungus of hair on their cheeks, because we all got thin in Guinea during that time, even the araucarias, even the aluminum waves of the sea, even the wind in the eaves of the buildings, reduced to a small crystal flute. The violence of explosions from mortars, bazookas, and recoilless rifles shook the lagoons of Bissau, dominating the March lightning. At night groups of colonists with pistols would go through the alleys threatening the shadows, black women would huddle in their huts quieting their children with their soft breasts, and no more on Sundays did people swollen with repressed desire sit on a bench in the small square with palm trees: they would linger in their rooms in shirtsleeves, with nothing to do, no place to go, covered with gnat bites, staring with distaste at the bed with uneven legs or the window facing the wharves where, instead of colonists, packets and caravels of soldiers were docking now, with the same frightened innocence of childhood in their eyes. One night they happened to hear on the radio, in a whirlwind of whistling, about the revolution in Lixbon, news, communiqués, military marches, the arrest of government figures, unfamiliar songs, and the next day the soldiers seemed less uptight, there was a letup in the shooting, blacks in sparkling glasses and holiday shirts had taken up positions on esplanades and squares in the place of whites. They called us together for a meeting at the Cine-Theatro used for tiresome zarzuelas and firemen's balls, where an artillery colonel with a triple row of ribbons on his chest climbed onto the stage where the orchestra was playing the national anthem enthusiastically and out of tune and he graciously offered them, with inexplicable generosity, the possibility of a free trip back to Portugal. A woman with gold capping her caries, divorced from a land surveyor who inch by inch, on his knees, had measured hills and streams, deceived in his calculations by the mineral repose of crocodiles, told in detail that there would be acts of vengeance, executions, shooting, searches. The officers with threadbare guts decamped from the ground floor and took the plane to Europe. Whole battalions, convulsed with amoebas and worms, with their quartermasters nodding from sleeping sickness right behind the band and the flag, climbed aboard rusty ships carrying their weapons and their dead. Barefoot guerrillas in camouflage dress, necklaces around their throats and with the cannibal breath of jungle cats, walked up and down the steps of the city massacring mulattoes with their bayonets. A bearded black officer, smoking a pipe, who didn't even say good morning to them, took over the ground floor, protected by a gang of thugs in berets, endlessly and frighteningly coughing and spitting on the sideboard with Macau pagodas showing on the demitasse set that had belonged to the late landlady. After a week had passed they called them to the Cine-Theatro once more and guaranteed them passage to the realme after hours of confused explanations in the course of which three majors in battle dress posted behind a table with the national coat of arms bellowed vehement speeches about the fascism that had killed us in the frying-pan sun of the Tarrafal concentration camp, about the ecclesiastical censorship by the police that had decapitated so many of our masterworks discovered in the most hidden printing presses, about the colonialism that even the pope had condemned in his closing speech at the Seventh Congress of Christian Esperantists with concerned words of apostolic preoccupation. The woman divorced from the land surveyor swore that the blacks, annoyed by the empty shops, were cooking the children of the city over a slow fire in field ovens. Soap and tobacco were in such short supply in stores that people were smoking mulberry leaves and the pages of herbal books, and they were scraping the grime off their fingers with steel wool. The ships arrived empty and left full, bulging with people and crates. Bissau was becoming depopulated of whites and the beginning of the rainy season found them not knowing what to do in a land of triumphant savages who shattered the blinds on the fronts of buildings with machine-gun fire. The ex-wife of the surveyor, who at the time was busy calculating the border with the Ivory Coast in inches, stopped seeking them out with her news of cookery and vengeance, and they found out that she was shacking up with a freckled guerrilla fighter from Bolana, shared with two more Fulas in an ill-smelling hut, plotting castrations and garrotings. A friend from the Gongorist sonnet factory named Jerónimo Baía described fearsome events to them, sodomy, poisonings, crossed rhymes, teams of prisoners in fetters driven into the jungle by blows from rifle butts. And when the tea ran out and every day they would dip the same tasteless bag hanging from the end of a thread into the boiling water, the wife, with her back to him, announced in her usual calm voice with which thirty-eight years before they had buried their baby girl: I don't belong here anymore.

The husband looked out the window at the lagoons of Bissau with their eels, the deserted estuary with no fishing boats, the roofs over which the stringless guitars of the thunder were playing, and he saw reflected in the glass an old man he took a while to recognize, because he would confront him only in the mirror for his quick Saturday shave and he paid more attention to the joints of his jaw than to the baldness, the wrinkles, and the other marks and devastations made by time, pulling on the iguana skin of his neck with a pinch of his fingers. The cruelty of the years grieved him like an unjust punishment, and when he turned to face his wife, sucking a remote memory of tea from his gums, he was indignant once more on noting with surprise the incurable erosion that time had brought on in her too, spoiling her legs with a marbling of varicose veins, making her eyelids puffy, her waist disappear, and he admitted with distaste We don't even belong to ourselves, this country has eaten up our fat and our flesh without pity or profit and they found themselves as poor as when they had arrived. That same afternoon he went up past the torn tapestries and oil paintings of the defenders of the realme in the government house, waited in the huge chair meant for a dignitary in the midst of dozens of whites and mulattoes for them to call his name, and a functionary in a jacket and wearing a dagger received him deep inside the building where it was filled with flippers and dismantled billiard tables, and after a difficult silence he requested two places in the hold for Lixbon. When he went back to the room his wife, sitting on the edge of the bed, was putting her hair into a bun with lots of pins. So he told her, dipping the little pouch of tea into a mug to top off his lunch, Twelve days from now we'll have a ship for Europe.

In the course of that time it rained ceaselessly, a storm that played like a harpsichord on the shutter tiles. The wind blew the mango branches into disarray, disorienting the azimuth of the birds, and the last soldiers were leaving, hunched over under the attack of the water. Polyps and tiny mushrooms burst forth from the folds in the sheets, in forgotten slippers, on the fringe of lampshades, on the very old wedding photograph with the bridal couple in front of a landscape of fir trees: the pair of us, me in my morning coat and you in your veil, so many years ago that they couldn't make out the faces, even though I still remembered the photographer's mustache as he disappeared behind the cloth of his camera and his drowned man's hand with a ring with a red stone on his forefinger that waved pleadingly at us For heaven's sake don't move now, look at the birdy, that's it, and they were terribly embarrassed facing that strange creature standing on three legs beside the zinc developing basin.

If the whites were becoming fewer in number, the blacks, on the other hand, were increasing in the houses stuck in the reeds alongside the rivers. They occupied the barracks that the army had abandoned, relieved of the weight of war and decorated with warlike phrases and the pictures of women in garters with opaline throats like art nouveau lampshades; they settled onto the benches in the garden, oblivious to the rain, with their Czech automatic rifles on their knees, hunting dogs for lunch; they posted sentries on street corners, drinking permanganate from drugstore jugs; they went in and out through the cretones of the government house, treading disdainfully on the tiles of power. The spittle of the bearded man's cannibals whistled wrath and orders on the ground floor, right beneath the back of our resting necks, and the woman said I don't belong here in a whisper that came from inside her disillusionment and misery, and she repeated softly I don't belong here in the exact voice of the bride in the picture. A large white packet was approaching the docks, threatening to destroy Bissau with the point of its bow where a carved mermaid with a huge pelvis split the foam with the golden fleece of her sex: we don't belong anywhere now, the husband answered, pointing to the ship topped with streamers, with royal emblems, bearing the standard of Admiral Afonso de Albuquerque at the top of the mainmast, difficult to discern over the cornices, the pulleys, the cranes, and the needle sprouts of the palm trees. They wrapped up the wedding picture and the small chest with mother-of-pearl swans in which age-old memories were gathered (a small sapphire ring, a pacifier, medals from Fátima, the thin profile of a little girl), the man put the money he had left into his dirty socks, and he lay down in his undershorts, aware of the rain that was disturbing his sleep, thinking about the windjammer that would carry them to Europe, with loose rigging under the dark, heavy clouds of Adamastors and dampness. As usual, during the last few nights, the wife remained for hours rolling around in the cataracts of the bedroom, recalling the hyacinths at her daughter's funeral, clinging to the iron bars of the bedstead with the tendons of her wrists stained with old-age spots. Don't forget the sewing machine, was the last thing the man heard from her before sinking into a jellylike coma where mirages of the past exhumed from the shadows floated. And the next afternoon, dry in spite of the graphite sky, they elbowed their way through the multitude of blacks who were crowding onto the docks in hopes of some barrels of fish or the consoles and cabinets that the stevedores might disdain. Because of the absence of rain albatrosses and blind albinos rose up out of the depths of the railroad cars to spin over the frigates with a swirl of howling. The stones of the harbor glistened with water or mingled with jellyfish, and they were taken with the impression that they could make out their bearded neighbor dispersing blacks with his pistol in order to clear the gangplank that a thread of passengers as aged as they was climbing up, holding on to the greasy railing. The sea was thickening around the propellers with a scum that aroused the voracity of the blindmen and the birds. The mango trees and straw huts of Bissau disappeared from the portholes. Cabin boys in striped shirts sailored along the yardarms, releasing the circus-tent canvas of the sails. The woman, in the lower bunk of the cabin, leaned her elbows on the sewing machine that a sackcloth cover protected from the hot embers of the waves. After three months of voyage, a small peach-colored sun peeped out amidst the granite of the clouds and right there they caught sight of the continuous bustle of Lixbon's Syrian market throbbing in the distance, castle walls, bonfires for Jews, processions of the flagellated, a simultaneous traffic of slave carts, cruisers, and bicycles. Ladies with unalterably kind smiles, with metal nameplates on their lapels, were assigning us to buses with three-diopter windshields that were parked along the waterfront and then followed along the kinks of the trolley tracks and the delayed defecation of coach mules up to the lobby of a five-star hotel near a convent school and a row of moribund acacias, and they proceeded to the desk by the corner of some sofas inhabited by Finns in beach shorts, to a chanted, fish-auction distribution of rooms.

After fifty-three years in a cubicle in Bissau, enduring mosquitoes and mist it was difficult for them to imagine the endless checkerboard of the marble floor, the wallpaper with hibiscuses, bellboys disguised as hussars from the French invasion, doors that unlocked all by themselves with the mysterious silence of starfish. The spacious cabin of the elevator, which whistled lightly along the orbit of comets, deposited them in a kind of basilica corridor with spaces for side altars numbered in silver ciphers. In the bed offered them, as broad as the sands of Bolana, the snouts of sharks swam over the starched sheets. A pontifical bathtub occupied the tiled sacristy in the neighboring compartment beside the Henry Moore sculpture of a toilet just for them, we who in Africa had shared our intimacy with that of other guests as we held back the level of our intestines, waiting for the flush of the one who'd come before us in the urgency of our necessities. Beyond the red and white curtains the buildings of Lixbon, church steeples, the isolated plague quarters, tiny gardens, and the sky, free of the storm clouds of Guinea, in which saints in tunics and clasped hands went up and down, gilded by the salt shaker of the sun. The old man placed the wedding picture on a ducal dresser without daring to associate the bride in a whalebone corset in the photograph with the septuagenarian with lusterless hair whose tics and gestures he knew almost to the point where words were absolutely useless. And yet, relaxing on the cushion of a dressing table whose mirrors were reproducing him with nauseating repetition, he touched himself for a long time to be convinced of his own age, making himself aware of the molars he was missing, the muscles that obeyed him with painful twitches, the face devastated by the Guinea climate ever since, at the age of fifteen, his father had sent him to the tropics under the care of a sergeant cousin who was falling apart from liquor and syphilis at a border garrison. Now the couple in the photo had turned into an iodine watercolor and we into worthless mummies startled by the dozens of little bottles in the bar of the suite, set out on mahogany trays with the restless immobility of chess pieces. At dusk they timidly entered the Alcobaça monastery dining room all dressed up in the clothes we'd kept during the voyage in the cord suitcase: my wife with the prehistoric dress from her old job as cashier in a buckle shop, and I with the chalk-striped suit à la Al Capone or a tango dancer worn for the first time at our daughter's baptism along with the ridiculous little tie, with the diameter of a shoelace, which was worthless in joining the two sides of a buttonless collar.

They placed us at the same table as three planters from Carmona who bemoaned their lost coffee and the memory of prostitutes in Muxima, a hippopotamus hunter capable of surviving for centuries, not moving a muscle, on the banks of the most inclement rivers, and a Goan fakir with an ascetic goatee who chewed nuts and bolts, perfecting balls of bread on the asparagus of his fingers. When they served the soup, a fat man in a bow tie raised the stool of an electric piano, pulled up his cuffs, with the rings on his fingers, and accompanied the chicken soup with hemidemisemi-quavers. Equerries with trays on their palms danced between the sideboards. The Infante Dom João's hunting mastiffs were devouring hares in the corners. And the husband noticed, fencing with his soup, that almost all the ladies were wearing red and white ribbons or mantillas or skirts where the print on the curtains was repeated. On some of them the tin rings from the drapes tinkled like joyless little bells and the younger girls, camp followers, the wild daughters of post commanders or students from nuns' schools that convent chauffeurs had led astray, wore them through a perforation in their lip or nostril, as when I first saw them swimming around the sailing ships with frightful shrieks. Almost at the end of the canned South African fruit salad that the discharged paratroopers left to ferment in the quartermaster warehouses in Lixbon, under pieces of uniforms, war medals, and catapults, a lieutenant with thinning hair combed forward from the back of his head in delicate goldsmithery crossed through the hibiscus tapestries from one end to the other with the monstrous birds in the room bowing here and there, making detailed recommendations to servants, and, after chatting for a moment with the artist of the quavers, who was fanning himself affectedly with a handkerchief, he adjusted the microphone to his height, blew a shapeless breath into it, said One two three testing, tapped it with his forefingers, bringing on a hail of stones, whispered to the piano in a bow tie who nodded yes and put his hands to the keyboard in a military chord, and then a divine, immense, authoritarian voice, coming not from the complicated hairdo of the lieutenant but from all points in the room, from the cupboards, from the vases with flowers, from the medicine vials on the tablecloths and the lips of the fantastic animals embellishing the edge of the walls, a voice from a garage or from a cliff, the size of the bombardments and storms in Bissau, informed them fiercely, ladies and gentlemen, informed them pompously, ladies and gentlemen, that they found themselves in the Hotel Ritz out of the purely paternal benevolence of the revolutionary authorities concerned with looking after the comfort and tranquillity of their children until the democratic State, born with the help of the military's midwife hand out of the rotten womb of fascist totalitarianism, which for so many decades had strangled and oppressed us, could get homes in prefabs or apartments in affordable neighborhoods for the victims of the now happily extinct dictatorship, and that in the name, comrades, of the class struggle and the building of socialism led by the political vanguard of the army, they would be punished on the gallows, by having their left hands cut off, by having their viscera pulled out from behind, or by being exiled to Macau in degradation for the intolerable abuses of frying sardines in washbasins, plugging up showers with pheasant legs, selling faucets designed by French architects to cachetic antiques dealers on the Rua de São Bento, the same as using the printed curtains of the hotel, I repeat, using the printed curtains of the hotel for blouses and adornments like those of a Moorish concubine.

After dinner, in the room, the man, leaning on the presidential magnificence of the windowsill that lacked only a cushion and a speech, for the first time faced the Lixbon night, murky from exhaust carbons, in the shape of a park going downhill toward a round square, and of trees coming together or separating in accordance with the inexplicable atmosphere of dreams, startled not to find huts or missions with famished novices and at the absence of the wormy-thigh smell of manioc on the rugs. The halo of the streetlights prevented him from making out the sky where the swampy ponds of Guinea overflowed with strange fish, guerrillas, and reeds hidden by the clouds of mist. His wife's phrase came into his head, I don't belong here anymore, and he thought that at their elephant age, retired, with no money, with no family, with no belongings, dependent on a small pension they wouldn't receive anymore, lost in bureaucratic pigeonholes or in drawers in the blacks' palace where moths and wasps were breeding inside closets and people shot by firing squads were sinking into the dahlias in the gardens, there was nothing left for them except themselves, the sewing machine suturing up time, the inlaid jewel box, I don't know what's happened to it, how about that, and the good sense to die from swallowing the whole package of tranquilizers the infantry doctor had prescribed for the migraine of nightmares, pills that tasted like limestone and had the virtue of pitching a person into the limitless waters of complete oblivion. He was getting ready to ask his wife Where did you put the pack of medicine I don't see it, what happened to those damned pills for total absence, when he heard her inside calling him from the absurd draperies of unbelievable silks, from the ostrich-feather pillows and the priceless furniture scratched with the penknives of former guests, and he found her standing, in a triumphant pose, leaning her hand on the rusty sewing machine surrounded by a web of threads, pieces of bedcovers, strips of drapes, and shreds of curtains scattered about on the floor. She was wearing a red and white blouse and skirt, identical to those of the other guests, and a belt where the brass rings from the windows were linked together. Her smile was at least as merry, malicious, and young as during the time of the wedding picture and their first moments of difficulty and affliction on the uneasiness of the sheets.

"They've invited me to a cat roast in the bathroom on the next floor," she said, pointing to the Bakelite toad of a telephone ready to move by dint of a pill from an inlaid box. "Do you want to come?"

The first friend they made at the Apostle of the Indies Boarding House slept three beds down, his name was Diogo Cão, he'd worked in Angola as an inspector for the Water Company, and when the mulatto woman had left for the bar in the afternoon he would sit down with me and the little one on the boardinghouse steps to watch the frenzy of the doves on the roof beams, and he announced to me in a now uncertain voice, sipping from a flask hidden under his jacket, that three or four or five hundred years ago he had commanded the Prince's ships all down the coast of Africa. He explained the best way to put down sailors' mutinies to me, how to salt meat, and how to sail with a keel, and how hard it had been to live in those arduous days of epic octaves and angry gods, and I pretended to believe him in order not to arouse the susceptibility of his drunken anger until the day he opened his suitcase in front of me and, under the shirts and vests and shorts stained with vomit and the lees of wine, I discovered ancient mildewed maps and a crumbling ship's log.

In the morning, while the mulatto woman was sleeping, anesthetized with anisette, snorting native-hut words from time to time, I would look for work in the neighborhood in order to satisfy the demented oaths of the fat man: I offered myself as an apprentice in the satanic hammering, with blood throbbing at the temples, at a locksmith's shop, or as a beginner in a butcher shop with gutted shoats that had girls' blond eyelashes; I tried to prove to foremen in checkered berets that I was just as skillful as street-gang Cape Verdeans in the use of a pickax to dig up the pavement, or to convince sanitary inspectors with the breath of sick cuttlefish that I could take better care of municipal urinals than the stumbling pensioners who sprinkled containers of caustic soda into stone drains where froth leavened and bubbled. Little by little, with the kid dogging his heels, he extended his fruitless search out to more distant zones of the city, near the lepers' district where municipal carts squeaked on their axles all day long; he proposed himself for cleaning the bothersome cartilages of the dead out of common graves in cemeteries; he tried, with a great effort and a visor cap over his eyes, to stand guard over great whales of automobiles in parks along the river patrolled by schooners of the realme, watching them slowly turning into corvettes; he searched out the alleys of the Sodré Docks, begging for work from the jack-of-spades doormen at whore bars; he ate rice cakes in lonely lunchrooms with a single stubborn fly on the counter; he passed a tangerine lollipop to the little one and climbed up to overlooks to impose himself on Germans as a guide to translate Lixbon's panorama of humble henhouses and tranquil poverty and cats licking the sun that was alighting on their rumps; he solicited, almost for nothing, the job of taking the slaps of mimics in the Coliseum while trapeze artists glistened up in the cupola, releasing virginal little clouds of talcum; and he would finally return, discouraged, to the boardinghouse, brushing a casual kiss on the mulatto woman who was coming down the hill all covered with sumptuous fish scales, crossing the vestibule where the lumbago of Mr. Francisco Xavier, the patron of Setúbal, was swaying like a metronome in his rocking chair, finally to sit down on the steps beside the drunken navigator, who was sketching on the ground with a small stick the likely latitude of islands to be discovered.

From the steps they would witness not only the arrival of the night that diluted house frames and revived dogs, but the departure of the band of Tagus nymphs in lamé that the Indian's mother shooed out through the weeds downhill in the direction of the discotheques on Arroios, the front of the morgue, and the duck pond in the Campo de Santana, skinny goddesses stumbling on pebbles and roots in the ground, pursued by their children with naked navels, who called after them, stopped, and went back into the boardinghouse like puppies returning defeated to the gates of country houses, and my wife was swaying among them on her exaggerated high heels, unavoidably damaging the gilded shoes that the fat man had made me pay for, increasing the debt and keeping her eternally tied to his pitiless pimp arrangements, so that what I owed kept growing like hairs in the nose and the nameless plants on rooftops, until the Water Company inspector calculated the money in arrears for me with the eyes of a person counting minesweepers on the horizon. It's so much, and he advised me to have a swig of the liquor in his bottle, The only solution is to stick a knife into the belly of that black bastard who's already bought two buildings on Morais Soares with your dame's little body and the sublease on a grocery in Penha de França, the fool getting richer and richer and me reduced to plotting islands and keeping my useless logs in a realme where sailors sit around scratching themselves, out of work, in pool rooms, pornographic movie houses, and café terraces, waiting for the Prince to write from Sagres and send them off in search of nonexistent archipelagos, drifting on the broad expanse of the sea. We would push back the drapes of the large room timidly and then he would say Discover the Azores for me, and they would be discovered, Find me Madeira, and, what else, it would be found, Land in Brazil and bring it here to me before some Venetian idiot takes it to Italy, and it was brought to him in the Algarve, where he was dining in the middle of a circle of physick doctors and bishops, that strange monster with carnivals, parrots, and banditry, to such a degree that when he saw it, so stupidly enormous like that, drawn by seventeen galleys and fourteen hundred teams of oxen, not counting the mules and Moorish slaves, that he stood apart from his people and asked me in a low voice, for a wise manne be hee and of goode understanding, What do I want something like that for when I've already got more than enough bothersome things? so he ordered us to put it back where we'd found it during siesta time, not even keeping a single parrot, and for us to forget at once the pellagra and the deaths we'd suffered in order to give it to him, and to the page who asked, pointing out the window, Milord, what nation is that? he replied, without hesitation, in his hoarse voice of a dry-land admiral that it was a sand spit from down the coast, my fine booby, you don't even know the shoreline, and with lots of Hail Marys and lots of work we did what he told us, that is, we towed Brazil back to America and whoever came along later could mess with it, except that we couldn't manage to hold on to the unusual parrots that flew shouting over the squares of Lixbon like a waving of colorful bath towels. Parrots on the weathercock of the cathedral, on the pointed hats of ladies-in-waiting, on the crenelling of Óbidos, and on the tips of erect penises, parrots that conversed in a language of émigrés like that of the women from the boardinghouse who go down to Arroios at nightfall, where beakers of medicinal alcohol and the arid monologues of old men awaited them, twenty or thirty mermaids in waves that glimmered like shad and platinum hair in the shadows, the flock of the patron of Setúbal, who was smoking his cigar peacefully, settled in his chair behind us in the vestibule. Two buildings on Morais Soares and me with no dinner, Pedro Álvares Cabral thought, to hell with freedom if this is freedom, what I want are my cabarets in Loanda and my mangy waterhole dawns, I want my damned native huts, I want the dunghill smells of my Africa, where I wasn't hungry or ashamed. The little one, enveloped in an aura of sugary orange, was solemnly licking a lollipop, Diogo Cão staggered from lack of sleep under his worn topcoat of a civil servant with back pay coming, so that at any moment he would have to carry the navigator, arm around his neck, to the room with syrupy breathing and *pacaça* emphysema, waiting for the mulatto woman to appear with the lights out, taking off the dazzling spangles of her low-cut gown, lying down on the bed with our son and me and falling asleep, alien to my male urgencies and the needs of my blood, and maybe squashed by the Indian against the jutting part of the counter, Hey, come over here, beautiful, show me what you've got under those lovely togs. I'd met her after the army at a railroad workers' dance, she wanted to be a hairdresser's apprentice, she was living in Vila Alice with her godmother, and we didn't court like a white man and a mulatto woman, but like a white man and a white woman, the two of us sitting, stiff, respectful, respectable, under the watchful eyes of the godmother, who was sewing endlessly, mending the tunic and trousers of a second lieutenant, with a tiny little bitch curled up over her slippers. There was a calendar on the wall that stopped at July nineteen thirty-five, daguerreotypes devoured by mold, oil lamps, images of saints, a clay sheep in the middle of the table grazing on its crocheted oval, until I can get enough money together for a house in Cuca, take five days off, and take you along with me for some sheets like these, I grow weak waiting for you, sunken in a sailor's bronchitis and going through wind-wards and leewards that I don't know and that worry me, through stormy winds, past unbroken promontories sought by the excited quivering of compasses. The rocking chair was groan-ing, the children had begun their usual crying in the perpetual darkness of the boardinghouse, and then and there, as best I could, up off the steps I lifted the admiral of the lost isles who was drooling winey spittle and sea chanties in a rotting voice, I crossed the vestibule with the hero of the oceans hanging on to my shoulder, said Good night to Mr. Francisco Xavier, whose gigantic belly was dancing this way and that, climbed the stairs, took the mariner's topcoat off him, his tie, his shirt, and when I tucked him into his bed I found a dead parrot drying out on the pillow.

In spite of a longing for Loanda and his home in the Alvalade district with a garden all around and engineers for neighbors, not to mention the apartment, almost never used, for European vacations at Costa da Caparica, Manoel de Sousa de Sepúlveda lived in Malanje in a two-family house a hundred yards from the military base in order to keep watch on the arrival of columns from the frontier: that very night little soldiers with frightened eyes or cautious lieutenants would knock on the rear door (settled in the living room, tense, with the radio off, he could hear their bootsteps on the paving stones of the courtyard), follow him through the kitchen, the corridor, the archway into the shadows of the bedroom on to the study, dimly lit like an oratory, with a desk covered by a dark cloth where the instruments for the ceremony were arranged: a set of scales, clamps, glass plates, magnifying glasses, flasks of reagents, a microscope, strange tools, little numbered boxes. The soldiers would take folded pieces of paper out of their wallets and spread the glimmer of tiny stones on the felt, items that had been exchanged for insect sprays or vials of quinine with blacks who dove into the River Cambo in search of crystals sleeping on the bottom sands. Manoel de Sousa de Sepúlveda, who was bald and widowed (his wife was resting her rheumatism in the cemetery of Lobito with a marble funerary angel, wings unfolded, placed on her chest so as to obviate any inopportune resuscitations), would drop onto a laboratory stool for a clinical analysis, light a flame that was more diaphanous than the face powder widows use, close his left eye with a jeweler's loupe, and proceed to the liturgical examination of the diamonds, almost all of them shards of bottles or fragments of carbon that he would push away with his spatula and a disdainful good-bye, while the panicky little soldiers or the officers with a worried cigarette in their jaws would cease their priestly davening, look at the collection of reagents and tongs, and, if some fragment disappeared into a damask box, leave happily for the main gate of the post. Manoel de Sousa de Sepúlveda would then put the jewel away in a sanctuary hidden by a slatted blind and wait for the Friday when his friend the PIDE inspector, a great big guy with a mustache who liked his spirits, would come to his house to dine on the usual rabbit in order to pass the contraband on to him, and the policeman, after tucking his commission into the depths of his pants, would send it on to Zambia via a trusted courier and the bald man would receive his little check from Holland or Belgium as soon as the stone fell into the fingers of an émigré cousin who was a lapidary in Amsterdam, with a goldsmith's shop in the red-light district where ladies of ill repute huddled in their windows like fleshy Buddhas. More important than the stones, however, and growing ever more important as the dust of loneliness gathered on the dead woman's clothes in the closet, was his taking the pruning shears out of the drawer, getting his straw hat down from the leverlike horns of the coatrack, hiding his face, even with the shadow of the hat brim, behind a pair of mica glasses, and as he pretended to be trimming the hedge with casual clips, watching the schoolgirls who went up the street at lunchtime, not noticing him, disappearing in whispering groups into the trees of the park, leaving behind the aphrodisiac of second-degree equations that battalion bugles swept far off with military dispatch. When he got back to his parlor the dead woman in the photographs was smiling her enervating, unchanging understanding at him from the sideboard with no sign of jealousy and the hake and sprouts he swallowed all alone in a room with heavy dark furniture like that of ancient abbeys had the taste of grammar lessons mingled with it. And he would doze off in a wing chair, thirteen-year-old girls running naked in his dreams.

One morning the bootblack in the café, in a voice down beside his shoes as he snapped the cloth over the tips, informed him that strange things had taken place in Lixbon: the government had changed, there was talk of giving the blacks their independence, just imagine, the cream-puff-and-toast customers were indignant. The return of columns from the Cassanje Lowlands grew more frequent and they'd lost their martial look, taking on the pacific physiognomy of commercial truck drivers: the bootblack probably wasn't surprised to see cradles and pianos sailing along through the hills toward Loanda. Manoel de Sousa de Sepúlveda heard the same talk in the barbershop, at the notary's, in the drugstore, and with his shoelaces gleaming he posted himself on watch by the boxwood hedge of his yard, straw hat on his head, observing the military post through the mica of his lenses. He witnessed unusual activity in the headquarters building, platoons of riflemen loading civilian panel trucks with cases of gunpowder and muskets, a whirlwind of yelling captains, medics gathering up water filters and antivenereal unguents. Because of some complicated business having to do with helicopters, he'd been in the Belgian Congo during decolonization and he'd learned how to sniff out anxiety and fear in the air, sense the hasty rush by the defeated warriors to dismantle things, types appearing and disappearing under the command of no one knew who and conspiring in native quarters, chatting with black priests, bandying innocent questions across pool tables. So he sold the house, the contents of the closets, and his wife's dresses to the owner of a Chinese restaurant for almost nothing, took up his shears to be aroused by the schoolgirls of Malanje for one last time, executed a sad hyperbole through the rooms, taking leave of the chipped kitchen sink and the gouaches hanging in the hallway, filled a suitcase with clothes, put his knee on it to close the lock, and the next week he was seen in South Africa taking the plane to Lixbon.

As soon as he set foot in the realme and picked up his luggage as it sobbed its way around the rubber baggage turntable giving little twists, he made a phone call from a boutique selling tobacco and craftwork (filigree seaweed, dolls from the Minhov region, small bottles of port wine, little kegs of egg nog, and Barcelos roosters) to the brother who lived in Lixbon, announcing Here I am, but since he had trouble understanding the reply, he pushed past a group of Australian nuns debating over martyr medals, opalescent virgins, and other cheap mystical doodads, settled into a taxi, and told the driver to take him to the Amoreiras Garden of his childhood. The straw hat and the glasses were probably still lying where he'd left them on the three-legged table in the vestibule, smelling of turpentine underneat the horned coatrack before which the dead woman, frightened by all those horns, would always cross herself when she came into the house, holding her shopping bag.

The brother, also bald, a sedentary customs clerk who had never been attracted to tropical adventures, continued occupying the ground-floor apartment that had belonged to their parents and where Manoel de Sousa de Sepúlveda had known a boring, slow childhood with a silk-merchant father and a quite fat mother who rolled the weariness of her asthma from hip to hip with painful movements.

Now, thirty years later, the old folks had disappeared with their double chins and smell of ribbons, carried off in a rush by an epidemic of bubonic plague, but the garden was just the same, surrounded by houses two or three stories high, most certainly inhabited by the same creatures as before, design teachers, retired naval officers who placed Chinese jars by the entrance for wet umbrellas, watchmakers with surgical fingers, dealers in coins, stamps, and eighteenth-century prints, types with canes who on summer evenings would settle down into the coolness of the alleys under the yellow moonlight of the plane trees or the arches of the aqueduct that runs along in the background, vaulting over the sloping street with its trolley tracks. The rest was made up of baroque bars and expensive restaurants, the stiff excesses of cognac, and at nine o'clock at night the garden looked like a painted stage set waiting for a performance that would never take place, with an aging actress strolling from tree trunk to tree trunk with her little dog who was all jubilant with his fraternal piss, the recess of a gravel walk, a few lighted windows, the startling pink halo of a dissolving September sunset: my boyhood here, concealed cigarettes, eager masturbation, a passion for inaccessible neighbor women, and street cleaners in salmon-colored vests hosing his childhood away.

The brother received him unsmiling with his napkin around his neck, grumbling, in the house from the past where in a disorder of theater wings decorations from ancient theatrical performances were accumulating, the impaled neck of a moth-eaten bull, dirty plates, porcelain, coatracks, the floor covered with newspapers (You'll have to pardon us, we're painting all this), and the study just as he'd always seen it except for the novelty of the television set on a table, and in the dining room the bald man and his wife in a shrieking argument over the work, watched over by an oil print of hares, radishes, and quails.

Manoel de Sousa de Sepúlveda settled down at a corner of the tablecloth on a folding chair, gathering the insults, looking absentmindedly at the doors with lilac frames on the sideboard, the cast-iron lamp with cobwebs on its wires, the dim emotions of days gone by when his father was alive and presided over meals in a museum silence. With the pretext of urinating he winnowed his way through the rooms, tripping over cords, pulling remote figures out of his memory, and he almost put his foot into a mousetrap between two cupboards with a crust of bread stuck onto a hook. Along the way he picked up his suitcase, went out through the stubble of turnip plants in the small yard in the rear, a few square feet of weeds and urban earthworms, went around the building, and came to the park walled in by the facades of design teachers who were snoring dreams of descriptive geometry on the T squares of their sheets. On the Rua das Amoreiras, with no drunks as yet, he negotiated the cost of a trip to the Costa da Caparica with the light of a taxi that danced along the trolley tracks. And during the ride he recognized without joy the almost deserted squares and avenues of Lixbon that followed one after the other with the monotony of an unfolding fabric: somber establishments, worn statues in the shadows, scrubby shrubs, the Basílica da Estrela, open for some wake or something, after that, from the bridge, the spice galleons anchored in the river, a ship with a cholera flag, and the stone masons at the Jeronymites who by the light of flickering firebrands were knitting together the lacework of the main archway.

On the opposite bank now, while passing the gasoline stations, Manoel de Sousa de Sepúlveda was startled by the gigantic sleeping animal hulk of the Costa da Caparica in the distance, the profusion of buildings, hotels, signs, the dim glow of cafés. Riding the trolley tracks he came across clusters of vacationing foreigners and the cars of émigrés, boutiques, discotheques, an unknown fever, and probably, almost certainly, no girls' school, no thirteen-year-old haunches on their way home. The taxi went around a circle near dunes and wooden huts and stopped a hundred or two yards beyond, on the edge of a street facing the smells of the sea and an expanse of sand crowned by the blue Nivea Cream ball set in the rusty skeleton of its frame. Reflected on the metal of the water, the poles of the awning looked like the antlers of buried reindeer, an army of shipwrecked reindeer, eyeless, hairless, that the tongue of the ebb tide had left on the shore.

The driver (nothing but shoulders, neck, hands, lowered eyelids like a saint in a niche in the rearview mirror) turned on the dome light so as to avoid any mistake in making change (a sign on the dashboard: I HAVE HEART TROUBLE, PLEASE BE SO KIND AS NOT TO SMOKE), and the structure of the inside of the car, a dampness of naphtha and rancid oil, came out of the shadows like old episodes that, oh my God, we want only to forget, cradle smells, watery faces, the terror of dying in one's sleep, his mother dragging her varicose veins through the pantry, or, closer in time, the years in Loanda and Malanje, his wife's death agony, the incandescent eyes of the diamonds on the felt, the whiskey guffaw of the PIDE inspector with his snout in a dish of rabbit and rice. They'd built a row of buildings beyond his and the Nivea Cream ball was the only star visible over the blackness of the sea.

He crossed the road, pushed a button, and the lobby of the building was full of imitation marble steps, of wall decorations, and plants sunken in an eclipselike light where the leaves in their pots seemed artificial, ocher and broad, like the ones you buy in fish-food stores, little cans with fins painted on their paper labels. And there were the two vertical tombs of the elevators, rising up like pious souls from landing to landing on their way to the chimneys on the roof from where the mouth of the Tagus could be seen and the barges on which H. M. the King Dom Fernando brought his court from Almada to Lixbon, the lighthouse, endless dunes, the lights of fishing lamps, and the windy silence of the sky.

He landed on the seventh floor into a tunnel that was a garden of doormats, each accompanied by its respective garbage pail, which the janitor had still not collected, and he stumbled along with his suitcase past strongbox doors with little peepholes at eye level so the tenants could see me small, twisted, and with absurd gestures, deformed by the lens, dropping his bag onto the floor, taking out the key, going into the tiny apartment that had a balcony overlooking the waves and the canoes, bought twelve years before with an eye toward retirement, toward an old age of cushiony leisure, watching summer sunsets, free of African swamp fever, munching solitary seafood at lunchtime in the submerged peace of Spanish galleons.

He pushed the knob, grabbed his bag again, turned on the light, and came upon five or six mattresses spread out on the floor, shapes covered with morgue sheets, boxes of canned goods, bottles of wine, and a man in his undershirt, his thin head of hair all mussed, rising up barefoot from a sofa with proprietary indignation, What the hell is going on, what's going on?

A child broke out into tremendous wails in the next room and some of the shapes in the sheets got up in turn, opening their mouths from sleep: two sandy-haired lads with the speckled lips of lambs, a ninety-year-old woman clutching a knitted jacket against her breast, a kid who stared at me with swampy eyes. The thin-haired man, standing now, suspenders hanging down along his pants, pointed his huge, square, accusing finger at me, repeating What the hell is going on, what's going on? in an endless offensive. And Manoel de Sousa de Sepúlveda noticed that even on the balcony individuals were snoring in woolen nightshirts worn as protection from the morning mist, stretched out on rugs, blankets, pallets, mats, on pneumatic swans, with noses pressed against the windowpanes like ghost sea basses. My masks from Loanda had disappeared from the walls, my mahogany clothes closets were gone, what's become of my leopard shield, I don't see it, where are the ivory elephants that they stole from me, where are the shelves with my fossils, my equatorial scarabs, my paintings of jungle clearings, because what I see now are clotheslines with Gypsy blouses drying, holes in the plaster, dishes with leftover meals, the smell of sour milk and a third-class railroad coach, the ninety-year-old woman in the knitted jacket spitting blood into a chamber pot.

The sandy-haired boys with lamb lips (where are my Austrian chairs, the aneroid barometer I inherited from my father, my butterflies from Moçâmedes, done in by a drop of acid?) advanced toward him, sliding along on the mattresses, each with a bottleneck in his hand, egged on by the thin-haired man who was slapping the innocent hairs on his chest, calling on the sea basses from the balcony to witness his misfortune:

"Did you ever see anything like this, by God? Did you ever see anything like this? If this isn't an invasion from the outside, what is it then?"

"This apartment belongs to me," Manoel de Sousa de Sepúlveda said to the expectoration of the nonagenarian (and my binoculars to spy on schoolgirls, and the candy I bought in Badajoz to tempt them with, and the irresistible artificial curls to make me look younger?) while he retreated, tripping over a bottle, leaning on a bench to straighten up again, muttering, thinking, muttering in a misplaced voice of defeat, "I bought it over eleven years ago, I just got in from Africa (and my dark glasses, and my straw hat, and the little lambs leaving school, and my diamond liturgy?), I'll bring the papers and everybody will see."

The sea basses on the balcony forced open the windows to enter the room, coming like smugglers on trawlers from the treacherous sea breeze that smelled of lobster and drowned men. An object broke noisily, the child screamed louder, and a woman's voice warned them from the bedroom that if you don't shut up I'll have to put up with the little bastard all night long. The thin-haired man, who was directing the turmoil, put his fat arms out toward me, irritated:

"You'll bring papers? Shit! You'll bring papers? What do I care about papers, the papers can go fuck: we're in a democracy now, dummy, buildings belong to the people living in them, the days of the PIDE are over."

"The guy says he got in from Africa, he doesn't know what socialism is," one of the sandy-haired boys defended me while the old woman, with dim eyes, was spitting into her pot.

"I told you you'd wake the little bastard up on me," the invisible woman threatened from my retirement bed and the electric alarm clock that would whisper love songs into my comatose ears at nine o'clock. "The first one to make any shitty noise can clean up the diarrhea he dirties with."

The thin-haired man looked for something to cover his behind with, sucked on the coal-colored teeth he had left, and ran his eyes over his resuscitated flock that was moving, wrapped in sheets like the silhouettes of corpses, giving off a smell of sewage and carrying with them the wormy whistling of the dark: they were the people with concave cheeks from the shantytowns of Fonte da Teiha, fanning the coals with straw to roast sardines, types who stole three square yards from the sea for a hut with planks that straddled fish fat, kale sprouts growing in the sand, and spikenard petals on the shore, hoboes with tight little striped jackets, aimless deserters lying on their backs in the underbrush, pine-grove prostitutes sticky with pitch, the survivors of broken caravels, and soldiers from faraway garrisons squashing lice on benches by the shore, dreaming about the slaughter of Indonesians and expeditions to China and threatening the police with outdated harquebuses.

"Take a good look at somebody who doesn't know what socialism is all about, an illiterate," the thin-haired man was saddened with sincere regret, pointing at me to the late-night wonder of his colleagues, who were beginning to take an interest in me, scratching scabs, scratching scars, scratching their runny eyes, taking an interest in my shoes, in my pants, in my necktie, in my suitcase, under the protection of the pageboy bottleneck swords wielded by the sandy-haired boys. "He's just arrived from Africa, poor fellow, he hasn't been here for a hundred years, he's been exploiting our little black comrades, he thinks the place belongs to him. This here belongs to the people, my friend, it belongs to the glorious vanguard of the proletariat, it was occupied in a revolutionary way, see? If you go to city hall you'll find my name there as the owner and agent of this rehabilitation center for people with spinal injuries, and the lout's still got the nerve to talk about documents."

"Shut up, damn it, show some regard," the woman howled from the bedroom. "Just when the kid falls asleep you start hollering out there."

And when one of the sandy-haired ones with lamb lips grabbed the lapel of his jacket, asking the ones on the balcony Have any of you seen the fine clothes closet belonging to this boob? Manoel de Sousa de Sepúlveda found himself in Malanje, pruning the hedge in the yard, waiting for the girls from the school. In the Malanje mist as it rolled through the trees in asthmatic exhalations, spying on the street through the imperfections of his glasses and imagining the bell for the end of classes, the books quickly closed, perverse fountain pens that are dropped and lost, the dirt road to the military post and then the paved street leading to their homes and me casually clipping branches and leaves, captivated by the dozens of young legs and waists going off.

"Have any of you seen this boob's closet?"

He imagined the briny mist of Malanje that wrinkles your forehead in mirrors and makes towels stink in trunks, he imagined the softness of the sky, the birds hidden like lines in the marshy membranes of the mango trees, the dead woman forgotten under her tragic angel, the schoolgirls whispering to one another, hugging and arguing on their way to lunch, and the shears clipping at nothing, clipping the air, clipping against their rusty warp the hanging drops of the mist, so he almost missed their pulling the suitcase away from him (Is there anything of value in this piece of shit? the thin-haired one was interested, tossing off a lock of hair that hung over his nose), the jacket, the shoes, fought over by a pack of pockmarked beggars, the wallet that they gave back to him relieved of the money and the Dutch checks, so he barely noticed the nonagenarian hovering about him, clicking her tooth, in search of her leftovers too, until they pushed him out the door, put him into the elevator, sent him back downstairs to the ground floor while the people from the Fonte da Telha were furiously dividing the treasure up above, and he paused in the lobby, out of it all, leaning against the mailboxes, with the bugles of the military post in his head, lighted by wall lamps, by the mist of Angola and by the light of the flowerpots, aimlessly crossing the avenue toward the beach after wandering blindly along the esplanades deserted by spider crabs, where the last workers were piling up benches and tables, the avenue to the beach, bordered by restaurants and fish stands huddling under the blue ball of NIVEA CREAM whose letters could barely be made out across the waters of the Costa da Caparica whitened by a small decoration of foam.

Manoel de Sousa de Sepúlveda became aware of dawn as the sun broke the African mist away from the roofs and balconies behind him, the shelves of the market, the waves of low tide along whose edge a pack of stray dogs was trotting, sniffing the excrement on the dunes, broken shoes, torn baskets, the reflection of a glass that burned like a mote in the eye. It must have been five or six o'clock in the morning and everywhere his eyes looked there were no traces of people on the sands: only broken-down huts, a supply shack, a trailer missing parts with curtains of leaves in the windows. Five in the morning and the waves, larger now, sending the dogs toward me as they swung the sad arcs of their tails. A thin Gypsy dressed in black popped out of the trailer and walked toward the water, smoking, a basin in his hand. The dogs grew in size, snorting like angry shoats. I settled myself better against the Nivea Cream ball and closed the neck of my shirt as if I were floating far above fear, far above anguish, above kidney stones, meals without salt, and the schoolgirls in Malanje. A cemetery angel with fallen bat wings crushed my belly, the peace of a sleepless siesta grew in his body. The Gypsy came back from the sea, the dogs' bronchitis was singing in my ears. Manoel de Sousa de Sepúlveda closed his eyes as the sun slowly began to color him.

"I'm going to sleep for a spell," he thought, hiding his ankles in the sand. "Anyway, I haven't got anything left for them to steal."

By the second or third week and after many discovery ships full of careworn eyes and baggage held loosely against the hollow of the stomach, the man named Luís gave up waiting for the refrigerator and the stove, most certainly stolen by Kaffirs in Loanda and sold to German plantation owners in Gabon, and he decided that his father, who was bubbling in the coffin with a fervor of worms, would have to content himself with a furtive burial at night in the shadows that cemeteries forget along the walls where the weeds are taller than the gravediggers' eyes. One of the guards who chatted with him at the end of the afternoon, watching the maneuvering galleys and the docking of caravels damaged by strange winds and commanded by ghosts in three-cornered hats hallucinated by coitus with sirens, offered him the remains of his lunch pail, that is, potatoes dripping with lard, banana ends, and chicken cartilage stuck to the aluminum bottom, the meal of a dry-land sailor cooked by a woman in a rear balcony in Beato grimy with her children's snot. The galleons, stripped of their sails, struggled in the morning through the oil from the Tagus trawlers to bear to the palace, much to its misfortune, a newborn penguin from the Strait of Magellan in a jam jar along with cases of ashtrays MADE IN HONG KONG from Sacavém. Here and there they were burning heretics on puppet-show platforms to please the people. An occasional Spaniard was killed for their entertainment. And everything else consisted of the pleurisy of locomotives, the usual gulls, and the pieces of anthracite left in the bushes by rats that had escaped from the ships where they fed on arrowroot cookies and the mummies of corsairs.

The corporal, who during breaks in his rounds settled down at his desk to decipher official orders couched in atrocious grammar with a great consumption of cigarettes, loaned the man named Luís the cardboard box in a corner where he kept the trash from maritime departments, newspapers from the Monarchie, trade winds, useless letters, the sunflowers from compasses looking for misplaced seaplanes, so a fellow wouldn't have to leave the area under his jurisdiction to wander through the city with a coffin on his back, looking for a cemetery where he could anchor the scattered shinbones of the dead man. They emptied it down an embankment by the railroad tracks where a wheelchair was sinking into the weeds at an angle, with its wheel in the air and they hauled the corpse into the halo of a streetlight surrounded by the carnival-costume flight of bats, their tiny mouths on target, grabbing scattering insects. They lifted the lid with its crucifix as a barge with galley slaves slipped down the Tagus toward Belém on its way to an unlikely epic over a sea of furious Neptunes, carpeted the insides with sawdust so the father, liquefied now, wouldn't drip through the cracks in the cardboard, each took his corner of the sheet and settled the stench into the box, muffled with more sawdust, rags, and the nylon cords from a mail carton while the rats from off the packets and stray dogs who had never been on board approached, sticking their whiskered snouts out toward the satins of the coffin that was exhaling the jellyfish odor of an ancient placenta until the guard, having enough of dogs, gave a kick to the casket, which went from the pier into the waters of the river, and they stood there watching it break up into boards, fabric, cotton wadding, and sheets of stearin, all swallowed up in the estuary quick as whiplash. A cart with actors was passing by two hundred yards away with a pandemonium of bagpipes on its way to a baptism at the palace, and there was the goldsmith Gil Vicente gesticulating in the midst of devils and shepherds.

So the man named Luís put his father under his arm and left, all powdered with sawdust, followed by a disillusioned cortege of dogs, straight to the first available cemetery in Lixbon and the baroque dwellings of the tombs that swarms of relatives cleaned with battery-run vacuum cleaners. He leaped over the bushes, driving away locusts with his sleeves, appeared and disappeared among the cones of the trees, disappeared around the corner of a cattle or freight car, returned at the level of the station platform and the neon tubes over deserted benches, and he disappeared again onto the Avenida Vinte e Quatro de Julho that ran along the Tagus and came out by the statue of the king on horseback, lonely in his square of ministries and arcades opposite the ferryboat dock.

The man named Luís switched his father to his other arm in order to relieve his elbow, but I really never thought that Lixbon was this maze of bay windows eaten by the acids of the Tagus, these sacred cows that are the herds of streetcars, these shops with little bags of almonds and bottles of liqueur, I really imagined obelisks, stone markers, statues of martyrs, squares where the wandering winds of adventure blew, instead of gouty alleyways, narrow streets with pensioners and nauseating warehouses, I swear I imagined a cove full of square-rigged ships bursting with nutmeg and cinnamon, and in the end all I found was a night of neglected buildings climbing up to a Carpathian castle hanging on the summit, a ruin with battlements in whose ivy the stagnant shouts of peacocks slept.

He trotted along the Avenida Vinte e Quatro de Julho in order not to lose sight of the railroad and the dull purpuric river awaiting high tide, with dozing locomotives, the crests of waves, and the smokestacks of cruisers on the right and on the left hazy gardens and streets with sanatoriums and people enduring the melancholy of their lungs at the windows, because he'd learned that Lixbon shuts up tight during dead hours into a somnambulant muteness pierced from time to time by ambulance bells or the discourse of a drunk wallowing in a flower bed in search of the best position to rest the heartburn of his intoxication. Streets with fountains of dray mules illuminated by the boxing-ring intensity of streetlights, streets with mulberry trees that cough up leaves, slanting Luciferian caves, the tuna-liver smell of the old man and no cemetery in the area, what a fraud, more squint-eyed buildings, more chimneys, more trains, and, little by little, as he approached the Sodré Docks, beer halls and flea-bitten cafés with tables for stevedores to play dominoes on, and on the other side of the avenue men-women with artificial malt-colored hair that depraved automobiles sought out, coming along in their low-cut gowns and rabbit stoles, clutching the straps of their patent-leather purses where they kept the powder to disguise their beards and the brushes to fix their makeup, drawing accent marks in ink over their depilated eyebrows. At the top of some stairs an old woman was lovingly gathering together stray cats around a package of leftovers.

Just before the square there was an increase in the little bars with zinc counters where the men-women could be seen inside, lying in wait, with painted flames, bars with gangs of rowdy women with mustachioed squires at the door in whispered wake-like conversations, and me with worms under my armpit, drifting through the city unbathed and without a change of clothing for more than a month, dry with thirst, feeding on leftovers, me, looking for the cedars of a cemetery gate, an area with crosses spread out through the darkness and inhabitants crumbling on oaken shelves. The man named Luís mingled with the resuscitated beings who peopled the shadows of Lixbon, scribes without falcon feathers in their berets, swordsmen in disgrace swallowing their beggar's soup in a corner, rabbis with greasy beards, a rabblement of seamen moving about the tables hawking contraband watches and fountain pens to fifty-year-old women who were enthroned over the linden tea of their retirement, Moorish bootblacks in stairways, their pockets full of brushes and cloth. The brass bands from firemen's balls playing off-key in the cockfighting alleys bristling with pickpockets and police. The men-women haggled over prices with the drivers of the cars, stuck their enormous heads in through the windows, trotted softly in the direction of a nearby boardinghouse, three floors of washbasins with a red light over the stairs to help the cross-eyed mole vision of people coming in. And discotheques like ships' boiler rooms and the sweat of the Tagus, for all occasions, depending on the manias of their customers, that bore the vestiges of sewers and lost places.

Borne along by a school of congers who were plucking sardine flowers from balconies with their teeth, he floated past the ministries on the Terreiro do Paço by the river, where cripples played sambas on their fiddles underneath the arcades and the breadth of the water opened up beyond the steps going down to the sea and the silk merchants and brandy shops on the Rua

Augusta. The transvestites with their African bead necklaces and their strumpet scarves had been left well behind, for this square at sleeping time belongs to the silence of an antique vial and the accordions of blindmen. One of them, his instrument on his back, marched along in front of me, waving his hurried little cane toward Santa Apolónia, the station with railroad coaches from the Frances, the Germanies, and the Belgiums, with a row of taxis waiting for passengers and baggage all around the enormous building, more monstrous than a barracks or a prison, where sounds break up on the cement. There inside, beside the boiling spouts of the locomotives that were leaving, was a circus spotlight, an esplanade at rest, émigrés nodding over bulging bundles and an attendant on in years sweeping up cigarette butts off the floor into an aluminum scoop. For a moment the man named Luís lost the blindman with the music who was tracking after his antenna beyond the station, so he ended up sitting down at a table on the esplanade with his father squashed down on the next seat, watching a female news vendor count the bills in her apron. If he went to one of the doors he would most certainly come upon the Tagus, that is, torpedo boats and dolphins and stevedores in print shirts and the bustle of disembarkation, the factories of Barreiro that were beginning to stand out as the horizon line grew clear beyond the rump of the hill. An attendant in a white jacket whose lumps and tears were accentuated by the cirrhosis of the fluorescent lighting leaned over me like a weary pietà and I ordered a quart of club soda where the bubbles leaped up from the bottom like insect eggs: maybe there was a sympathetic cemetery in some break in the disarray of dove cotes and roofs of Lixbon, with television antennas attached to the headstones of the deceased, and at that moment he came to notice the blindman, guided by his lively cane, trotting along the platform by the limited to Oporto, but looking more closely he saw it wasn't he but some switchman with a cap on his head, armed with the long crowbar used to change the direction of trains. The attendant, with no customers on the empty esplanade, came over to sit down at a table six feet away, taking a pack of cigarettes out of his pocket, and the man named Luís was surprised at his buccaneer's face and soft body, curled into round folds, waiting for his morning coworker.

The two of them, side by side, with the dead man in between, watched the arrival of the platoon of cleaning women who disappeared, shuffling in their slippers, into a kind of hotel windscreen. A begging couple wearing shoes without laces, with plastic bags hanging from their fingers, lay down on the slats of a bench to rest from their endless pilgrimages, with outstretched hands. A set of railway cars went off howling into a distant tunnel, and I thought Any moment now they're going to turn out the lights and I'll see the redness of dawn in the windowpanes of the building fronts, the ugly office buildings out there topped by stovepipes and inhabited by funerary worms. We remained there, the attendant and I, in that boundless expanse of railway cars in a garret silence that the blindman's cane cut as it went back and forth with its endless tapping. The lights had dimmed a little and the river swelled up over the side entrances without boats or birds, crested and wrinkled like the bottom of a shallow pot. A voice announced the express from Paris over the loudspeaker and a hubbub of émigrés on vacation, stultified by the torpor of the trip, limped off toward the taxis arranged in a diminishing line beside the office buildings. The man named Luís caught sight of the blindman in the confusion of passengers, right in front of a gentleman in a topcoat who was pulling a child by the arm, he heard the Morse code of the tip of his cane on the cement, but the man in the topcoat disappeared as he passed near him, blended into a group with suitcases on their backs stumbling for lack of sleep. The esplanade attendant, forgetting his ballpoint and order pad, got up like an accordion opening up and slipped sidewise into a kind of booth or kitchen: I'll bet he's going to turn out the lights, I thought, I'll bet he's going to close everything up now that the Frenchmen have arrived, close up, check the locks, leave, abandon me to myself and the blind-man in this garage of echoes and vapors. Then I took the bottle of soda water over to a corner of the table, grabbed the boneless attendant's pen and notebook, settled better into my seat, leaned my left elbow on the tabletop, and with the tip of my tongue sticking out and my brow knitted with effort, I began the first heroic octave of the poem.

God knows that I didn't want to, God is intimately aware of my flesh, the reason for my sins, and the labyrinth of my intentions. God has been with me since India, where my father worked out of a bivouac as a messenger of the customs service and my mother cooked the luncheon turtle in the lean-to in the rain, and he's stayed with me over the years that came after, bending the palm trees on the beach during monsoons with just a single finger of his wind and lowering a full-fledged night right down in the middle of the day as it transformed iguanas and women-kind. God took me with him to Mozambique as the servant of a marquis who was returning to the realme in a schooner with sails puffed out from the fans of ladies-in-waiting, weighted down with oriental baubles sold afterward in subway passages by skeletal gurus squatting on the floor beside a fifer and a box of cigarette papers. The night before my departure from Lourenço Marques I spent in the slum bedroom of a Chinese woman I'd met two hours before levitating along an avenue in the Baixa with short little steps, and when I awoke I saw through her mute smile and through the window the fans of the ladies-in-waiting waving on the horizon and a centenary mandarin kneeling on a pillow and lunching on beetles out of a Barcelos bowl. For several months, my dear Christians, I drank tea and chewed geckos in that room where everything (pillows, domestic utensils, pictures, and cruet holders with soy beans) stopped two feet off the floor, except for the cracks in the walls and the paper stripping of the blinds, and where the mandarin would bend in my direction in deferential bows from morning till night before unrolling at our feet the mat on which he slept, with dragons who stuck out their tongues on the fading straw.

The slum, almost at the water's edge, was inhabited by water birds that roosted on the sheeting of the roofs and people from Macau in wide-sleeved tunics fumigating essences destined for the gods on the streets, with pigtails hanging down the backs of their necks and who live on the bottom of dishes amidst willow trees and pagodas. The only white man in the neighborhood sold bibles, erotic postcards, and record players from door to door in the city, his name was Fernão Mendes Pinto, he owned a hut on the sand that was crammed full of equinoctial junk and memories of Malaysia, he would sit at the edge of the water, inspired by the sunsets, he made me a partner in the gospel business and one afternoon when I got back earlier than usual to the slum because of an insidious attack of sinusitis, I found him, naked and repulsive, on top of the transparent little frog of a Chinese woman, who was smiling at the ceiling with her unalterable sweetness. The mandarin, surrounded by sticks of incense, was contemplating the drizzle through the holes in the adobe. Fernão Mendes Pinto, without stopping his work, waved Good evening to me, snorting, and only when he'd put on his long johns, his beard still mussed and his hands unsteady, did he show any interest in the number of Gospels sold. Three, I answered, coughing because of the fog from the incense, and with my percentage of zero point two of the profits I set myself up on my own in Beira and was bogged down month after month in the swamps along the shore, pursued by pagan arrows, until I stumbled upon a stone marker covered with vines in the middle of a grove of linden trees. Figures in rags were wandering among miserable thatched huts and just then a whistle coming from the interior cut the jungle in two and, breathing with anguished emphysema and giving off black smoke over the treetops, the five o'clock railcar appeared.

With the railcars there was an unceasing arrival of politicians, paving contractors, mayors, and tax collectors. The very next morning the local radio station (built overnight by stonemasons secretly piled into the boxcars) thundered over the city with a program of light music sponsored by a syrup for infantile tapeworm. A sudden village of dwellings, supermarkets, and movie theaters smoothed down the dunes and advanced in terraces toward the forest. They set up the stone marker, cleaned of leaves, in the basement of a museum in the shadow of wax busts of memorable explorers. They organized a naval club for paranoid commodores in an abandoned lugger after freeing it of the skeletons of caulkers that broke up into dust as soon as the palm broom touched them. The pagans, tamed by gunfire, worked as cashiers or stokers, or they went out fishing in Danish canoes, surrounded by the ghosts of icebergs. Circuses began to disembark from freight cars and tightrope walkers set up their nets in squares stolen from eucalyptus trees and weeds over the pineapple-colored shoes of august personages. From time to time the governor, attended by mustachioed officers, would visit the slums, promising sewers, and he would leave in a huge automobile with flags alongside the hood, holding a young goat in his braided arms to the sound of the national anthem.

By that time I was already living in the shack in the slum on the side facing the bay, which the sea winds didn't reach with their hint of dead sperm whales and the smell of delicate sirens' teats, and where a sort of orphan sadness rained down incessantly. I'd married the white merchant's adolescent daughter after convincing him in a parlor devoid of furniture with half a dozen persuasive banknotes and had mentioned that the authorities would certainly be interested in that small traffic in savages between Nampula and Beira, and three years later, almost to the day, that communist business of a military revolution happened and I made a deal with my partner in the wooden-idol business, turned the woman over to him, received an airline ticket in exchange, left those flea-bitten hovels of Pakistanis, and took a seat on a plane to the realme.

At first I didn't know what to do in an absurd place called Lixbon, with no marmosets on the beaches or hippopotamuses in bathtubs, a capital, my beloved children, lacking in tobacco and cotton, more ancient and quiet than a paralytic aunt, whose doors and windows climbed up and down hillsides, blinking their chintzes at an anchorage of hydroplanes manned by Gago Coutinhos in sheepskin jackets. Lying on a park bench, unable to fall asleep, it was hard for me to get used to the absence of sapateira plants in the monsoons, replaced by cathedral domes, the pyres of saints, and gouty fat women. Then he began to beg for alms here and there on Sundays in the vicinity of churches, dressed in the shreds of a cassock and the clothes of a castaway he had fought over with other drifters on the Terreiro do Paço as the waves broke up the ships worn out by diarrhea brought on by bananas or armadillo meat returning from Brazil against the seawall.

On the eve of another ordinary day, searching at night in Campolide for paper and chicken bones in garbage pails, he ran into Fernão Mendes Pinto again as he was coming out of the wild depths of a Cape Verdean discotheque right under the patent-leather purse hanging from the armpit of a mulatto woman submerged in acrylic foxes. He was earning a living now from a constellation of residences and boardinghouses for Africanist gentlemen down on their luck, and he was planning to branch out with his business, exploiting the lowdown neighborhoods of Intendente, the Avenida Almirante Reis, and the Mint, near bars and dubious dance halls where the lights brought up out of the shadows, to the rhythm of the music, bits of protuberant faces that were like fish out of a basket. He explained all that to me on a first-floor apartment of the Arco do Carvalhão with crocheted doilies on the easy chairs and an inlaid fisherman in a checkered blouse, dragging his net over a sideboard, while the mulatto woman, who was taking up a whole sofa with the spangles of her behind, was spreading out the cups of her fingers like frogs in a cistern. Along with the fisherman there were souvenirs everywhere of trips to the Orient, Japanese lanterns, divinities carved out of limestone stalactites, a fragment of the left lung of the Buddha in a hospital test tube with an adhesive-tape label, and a lock of hair from an Etruscan prince, enclosed in a copper medallion case. Fernão Mendes Pinto showed him the pile of paper already typed up dealing with his extensive voyages (Someday I'm going to turn all this junk over to a publisher), took a bottle of Drambuie out of a cupboard filled with cartilaginous jellyfish under the sentimental oil painting of a weeping boy, and with the eighth drink invited the patron of Setúbal to run one of the branches of his enterprise, a run-down building behind the Military Academy, and I'll bet it won't take you a week to get it into the shape it ought to be in.

Mr. Francisco Xavier began by transferring into those afore-said walls his descendants from innumerable concubines out of lechery and ignorance, for, my dear brothers and sisters, God had long ago designated me as his chosen one, which descendants slept with my sweet and understanding mother under Dom João V's aqueduct, which carried water to Lixbon, enduring eternal colds from the drops that fell on them from the stones, slipping perfidiously down the numbed channel of the napes of their necks. Unemployed friends, penniless drunkards, and rummagers in trash cans helped me repair the walls with pieces of cardboard and remnants of tiles, stolen beds, toilets, and disemboweled mattresses from junk shops and carried them through the city at night in a procession of contraband to the disbelief of doormen at bars who were frightened by the fluttering flight of night tables. Four days later he crossed the city on foot, overcoat down to his heels, to inform Fernão Mendes Pinto that thanks to half a dozen promises made to the Most Holy Virgin and the little shepherd girls of Fátima, the Apostle of the Indies Boardinghouse was ready to receive any sinners who might appear out of the tropics. He found the buccaneer, wearing glasses, in his bathrobe, seated beside the little Nazaré statue and his innumerable useless objects, editing the account of his deeds with various colored pencils. The entrepreneur cleaned the filter of his cigarette holder with a blotter.

"Very good, my little friar," he said, involved in the events surrounding a massacre of Chinese. "On Saturday at least six airplanes and two frigates are arriving from Guinea: with this rigamarole of democracy they're running away from their holes like rats."

Accompanied by the mulatto woman, he took on the job of talking to the owners of clubs on Arroios himself, adding up figures on paper napkins, so they would accept a future flock of Tagus nymphs, he supplied me with seven dozen lamé dresses and three boxes of antivenereal pomade, rouge, face powder, eye shadow, and hairpins, he approved the rooms, nodding his head, and declared as he left, going downhill kicking stones, The day after tomorrow I want at least twenty-five ladies of the evening working down there.

If proofs were necessary, the absolute certainty that God is with me is that on Monday I sent, all decked out with spangles and shawls, thirty-eight African women to the discotheques on the Avenida Almirante Reis and Martim Moniz, not to mention, oh, servants of the Lord, the ones who spread out their languid hips through the parks and courtyards of the city from Belém to Ajuda, smoking patient Marlboros as they strolled along. In no time, and thanks to the blessing of Our Father, a far-flung flock of women converted to the Faith occupied all the neighborhoods of Lixbon all the way down to the Alcântara docks, where the air was like cellophane in July, and with their irresistible perfume assaulted the marine guards of NATO squadrons or the crew of Christopher Columbus, deranged by beriberi and strange landscapes. And yet, in spite of the prosperity of his enterprise, Mr. Francisco Xavier, settled in his rocking chair, still maintained inside himself the ulcer of the abandonment of his wife, whom he'd traded in Mozambique with a centenarian who stank of a stable.

"Why don't you go fetch her up from down there?" Fernão Mendes Pinto asked on one of the first Fridays of each month when they checked figures and divided up percentages under the tutelary eye of the fisherman who was pulling the net on his piece of furniture. "Maybe the old man has died."

Mr. Francisco Xavier bought a colonial suit of clothes and a footlocker from a family of Gypsies who were crossing the Paço da Rainha in a caravan of tatterdemalion carts with mules quivering from hunger and coughing on the shafts. He offered one of the younger mulatto women to a captain of Dom João de Castro, who was sailing for India with an aim to conquer Diu, and while they were fitting the ships with kegs of gunpowder and large bronze cannons with hand-sculpted martial bas-reliefs done by goldsmiths who had lingered over detail, he bided his time on Intendente, chatting about Asia with distracted whores who were paying more attention to the interest from automobiles than to the tedious theory of catapults, and right there I obtained passage on a warped trawler that made several stops in Africa in order to bury in the sand the lookouts who'd died of plague and take on boxes of peanuts, a dozen live cows, and a colonial platoon of variegated natives supplied with armored tiger skins and curare blowguns. Mr. Francisco Xavier escaped under the cover of the coming and going of stevedores and continued on to Beira, borne on the shoulders of a huge black man who years before had protected Mouzinho de Albuquerque with nothing more than the simple presence of his biceps. In the course of a stormy trip lasting five months and three days they crossed paths with disheveled garrisons delousing themselves on the beach, missionaries who were explaining the mystery of snow to Hottentots by the use of extraordinary comparisons, one of the Magi astray on his camel and searching the sky, with its countless twinkles, in vain for the star of Bethlehem, trunks

washed up on shore full of naphtha balls and overcoats, and sirens crucified on reefs with cockles in the place of hearts until
they reached Beira as it tipped toward the ceramic rainy-season
sea, the palm trees on side streets that opened onto the harbor's
smell of salt and steamship oil, columned buildings inhabited
by the silence of times long gone by, by parasites and worms on
rosebushes, not to mention the locomotives that cut through
the curtain of the jungle and snorted alongside us like rhinoceroses. Mr. Francisco Xavier dismissed the black man, who immediately disappeared into the glowworm taverns in the workers'
district, where he slept with six women at the same time, and
he went off to the disconsolate clearing of tin huts and circus
trailers, far from the waves, and which the new buildings had
already begun to devour, in search of that little piece of yard belonging to my partner and the turnips treasured by snails' molars. His hobbling soles, oh, people of God, recognized the pits
in the pavement. Boys with thread-thin limbs were having fun
in drainage ditches, playing secret games. The drizzle was pecking noiselessly on grass roofs.

The patron of Setúbal took several turns around the clearing, disoriented by new huts, unexpected steps, faces and trash
heaps that he didn't know, the beginnings of a cemetery beyond
the last tent where eight rows of wooden crucifixes were lined
up in the weeds. Asking directions here and there, he was drawing close to the citron and young-mare smell of his wife's body,
which he finally discovered in a gathering of stray cats, living in
a canvas structure inside of which the white woman, barefoot,
squinting through her eyelids swollen from smoke, was stirring
the soup in a nauseating pot. Cans with begonias, still with their
old cocoa labels, were withering in the oval of a window. My

partner's street stand with handicraft knickknacks was covered with caterpillars in a corner. When I pushed the door and the joints of the hinges yielded and leaped, the woman looked at me without surprise, concerned with the boiling soup.

"Is that you?" she said, pushing away the curiosity of a chicken with her heel.

She'd aged so much in those months that she now looked like those grandmothers in photo albums whose mingled wrinkles and inexplicable eyes seemed to come from strange countries on the other side of the moon where the most transparent of objects are understood backward and an upside-down language without vowels is used. Contact with my partner (reproduced, furthermore, in sepia on a shelf, with the frame cut diagonally by a black mourning band) had turned her flesh yellow, dulled her skin, hardened her with bunions along the edges of her slippers, and Mr. Francisco Xavier was face to face with a creature of indeterminate age chewing mush with the sponges of her gums, angry at the hens who would forget their eggs in the straw of the mattresses. She'd lost her majestic hips and lower back of days gone by and tufts of grayish hair were sprouting on her legs. The usual rain was falling in the alleys with cats where an occasional venerable member of the Chinese circus, stupefied with drink, was staggering along in his patent-leather leggings. Mr. Francisco Xavier pulled out from under the bed that was still soaked with the dead man's malaria a first-mate's chest and he idly searched in the hut for the white woman's threadbare clothing as she stared at him with empty inertia over the light. He gathered together skirts, low-cut boots, two blouses, a hairbrush that lacked some bristles, an enameled cigarette case with rings and tortoiseshell bracelets inside, a thread with the rusty nose of St. John Brito, dumped everything into the felt-lined chest, and fastened the heavy metal catches. Then he handed his wife a smock and some slacks, ordered her Get dressed, took an umbrella with the handle in the shape of a dog's head with marble eyes, opened the broken ribs, and when he returned a half hour later, dripping with the clover perfume of winter, he'd fobbed off the house and cheap statues on a trapeze artist who still had some money left for his nighttime wine. His wife was waiting for him, sitting on the trunk with a neutral calm on her weary cheeks.

"Where are we going?" she asked in a sick voice along which the syllables stretched out with the languor of worms.

Holding the handle of the umbrella over his head, the patron of Setúbal looked her over with disdain in his eyes, at her dactylic mouth, her breast that had no ardor, her slack stomach, and her lamb's hips, before dropping pompously onto a leather stool.

"To work as a whore in Lixbon," he informed her as the dirty water ran down the coattails of his jacket. "My mother ought to be able to make something out of you."

When Vasco da Gama arrived in Vila Franca de Xira by van, with the poker deck in his pocket, aiming to find work at the cobbler's trade, instead of the trees and houses and streets he'd remembered at night in Africa with the meticulous precision of longing, he found a land that extended beyond the rooftops and the pagoda of the bandstand submerged in the vast spread of the halted waters of the Tagus, drowning farms, cows, and walls and driven by November rains. Families clinging to the tops of poplar trees saw passing by, adrift in whirlpools of mud, the bloated bodies of bureaus, mules and dogs, double basses lost to their clefs forever, women with their fingers motionless in sewing gestures, and mugs that said SOUVENIR OF LOULÉ while they awaited the unlikely help of firemen's launches. The van stopped safely, after avoiding cascades, tributary streams, and loose stones, on a hillock where a northeaster heading nowhere was burning the roots of bushes with sulfuric odors, the passengers got out, feeling along the uneven slopes with the soles of their shoes, and the pensioner, patting the playing cards in his pocket, immediately distinguishing the wild jacks of useless suits with the simple inspiration of his finger, settled himself on a rock to wait for the river to abandon the town slowly with an ebbing that was like swallowing saliva so the band could recommence an interrupted waltz on the stand, people could walk through the streets again, druggists and herbalists could draw back the netting that covered their windows, and the calendar, at rest, could start working again, beginning with some fortuitous Sunday decided by the mayor's finger blindly pressing onto a mosaic of numbers. The nephew in the shoe store would come out onto the balcony to greet him with his ceremonious, habitually pale eyes of a convalescent pony, he would recognize the primary school, the music academy, the bull ring, the market square, the pool with grayish newts in the unfinished maritime museum whose plans had been grounded for centuries in the drawer for things to be done where the section head kept his luncheon salami amidst the reports of engineers, and he would spend the whole night in the café in the center of town in a fierce game of cards with the notary's clerk, who would play his aces ahead of mine and pitilessly outguess my queens, witnessed by the silent radio and a cluster of astounded spectators.

"Hell," he consoled himself, watching the retreat of the Tagus with hate, "in spite of everything they made me a count."

And he remembered when they'd called him to the Palace, given him a fleet, and sent him off to India, providing him with the help of a bundle of maps of invented continents, stacks of lying reports by foot travelers, and a little Capuchin friar with a hair shirt and a rosary in his fist, vested with the specific task of blessing the dying. He remembered Restelo in the morning at the moment of the departure of the sailing ships, the court arranged on a platform with a fringed awning, watching him take off, the ladies-in-waiting whom he pinched surreptitiously in the palace garden as their pumice smell mingled with the queen's essence of passionflower. He remembered the bishops in gold vestments, the apostolic nuncio and his dark glasses of a taciturn mafioso, the wives of ambassadors from distant lands with their low-cut gowns, the market watching the weighing of anchors with awe. He remembered the crows who recited the *Hino da Carta* in taverns, he remembered the people, alas, the people, waving little green and red flags, the old woman who threw me the bony blessing of a prophet as they were already sailing with the wind toward the currents of the river mouth, but he had to wait for thirty-one days on his stone atop the hillock, playing cards by himself with infinite calculated mistakes and dilatory maneuvers, unable to win or lose, until the Tagus returned to its bed and Vila Franca arose whole out of the mud, the drifting corpses, and the broken mulberry trees, just as he had preserved it inside himself during fifty years in Africa, having forgotten now about the begging watercolorist who had sketched it for him and the other captains at the moment of their departure, in uniform, like members of a handball team before a decisive match.

With the retreat of the flood, the settlement, of which only fragments had been visible through the ocher layer of water, took on its usual look once again with no transition and halfway down the hill Vasco da Gama began to hear the hammering and the gunning motors in garages, the sounds from the school playground, and the typewriters in government offices at the same time that an elderly music lover climbed up the steps of the bandstand, settled into an iron chair, took an ancient clarinet out of his case, and all by himself in the center of the music platform began playing a waltz as light as the hem of a dress, raising his chin from time to time to the maestro who wasn't there. The bloated oxen returned to their normal dimensions, grazing on the grass beside the river where the small rowboats of eelers were tying up and Tagus nymphs were coming in the afternoon to fix the algae buns of their hair.

Drawn by the fifer's insistent waltz, the count entered the town like dead people in dreams, recognizing door knockers and details of masonry and astonished at neighborhoods that had come into being during the course of his absence as a navigator in the Orient, modest blocks that smelled of barley soup and widows' weeds, the disjointed swaying of daisies and housing grants, without any *pau-de-fileira* for the belching of drunks. Power lines crossed the sky, all ready for birds' eighth notes. And there was the novelty of blacks who'd come from Guinea and Angola, pedaling on postal service bicycles in messengers' uniforms.

The cobbler shop that he'd left when he'd emigrated, in the shape of a niche stolen from bats' coital activities, now occupied a whole block, with show windows capped by a neon sign, and inside were dozens of clerks kneeling like vassals before the socks of customers ensconced on yellow velvet thrones. A dignified lady was going on with her tinkling calculations at the cash register whose drawer sprang out with devilish leaps. The nephew, in a double-breasted jacket of *Covilhã* fabric and a pearl teardrop in his necktie, dressed as if going to an undertakers' ball, was presiding, hands behind his back, over a flurry of low boots, and it wasn't to his liking to see before him that mossback of a great-grandfather with a sword, and he showed him a room in the rear of the establishment with a skylight in the ceiling and a thread of withered light trickling through like water, spreading out over the cracks on the floor, on the condition that he wouldn't lower the family prestige by exhibiting his sidewhiskers of an ancient Neptune on the streets of Vila Franca. Vasco da Gama, without being offended (Not even that boob of a king thought I'd come back), tested the wire spring of the bed with his knee, piled on the table hardtack necessary to get through the tumultuous passage of long seafaring nights, and forty-eight hours later he was seen in a lunchroom fleecing unwary farmhands with his cards. In that way he won a plow, eighteen horses, a herd of cows, mismatched harnesses, a bound Berber grammar, a furnished flat in Canecas, several choice bullfight seats, and even the firemen's ambulance, which had been obtained by public subscription, by defeating by half a point in the last round the head of that organization with a magical five. When the nephew saw him bring the animals in through the revolving door of the store in a pandemonium of cowbells, terrifying clerks and customers in stocking feet who were scaling the shelves up to the top as fast as they could, when he heard the awesome siren of the ambulance parked in the entranceway, he suggested to the navigator that he purchase the products of his winnings on the condition that he immediately undertake a second voyage to India with the hope that the octogenarian would succumb on the Isle of Loves, worn out by a swarm of insatiable nymphs.

The count, however, fed up with storms and pellagra and sick and tired of curing venereal diseases from Goa with acid baths that skinned his scrotum and hindered his walking for weeks on end, had taken a fancy to the town of his adolescence, which the tides of the Tagus revealed and hid with a magician's legerdemain and to the bell-cows grazing on heels, taps, and tissue-paper wrappings under the infernal noise of the ambulance. He'd acquired the habit of riding horseback in the afternoon through the main squares in the region, showing his cards and challenging strangers to duels of blackjack, and in that way he'd become owner of the butane factory, the electrical plant in

Cartaxo, all the cement mixers in the region, the funeral parlor, seven cattle-breeding stations, the Misericórdia hospital, and most of the commercial establishments between Tomar and Santarém. He conceived the fearful plan of taking over Portugal, borough by borough and city by city, with his luck at cards and his delirious jurisdiction extended as far as Portoalegre, where he controlled the tribunal and three-quarters of the aldermen, when the king Dom Manoel, pressed by the concern of parliament, summoned him to Lixbon and gave him the news that he'd named him commander of an expedition of Sudanese biologists being sent to the North Pole by submarine in order to study the genetic laws of the reproduction of penguins.

Forty-two years had passed since Vasco da Gama had last spoken to the monarch, and after uncounted months in the antechamber, reading doctor's office magazines, mingling with executives in vests, astrologers in star-speckled capes, representatives of majority, minority, and nonexistent political parties, an Italian journalist, and a delegation from the bakers' union, encased in the powder of their morning flour, he found an aged prince shooing away flies with his scepter, a tin crown with glass rubies on his head, and the applesauce halitosis of a diabetic huddled on the seat of a Gothic window that opened out onto the galleons of his squadron, which he was contemplating without interest in the melancholy of his flu. The Jeronymite monastery, finished decades ago, had immediately been transformed into an archaic monument given over to Sunday weddings and the pathetic celebration of defunct glories, where thin-soled pumps echoed on the concave paving stones in an explosive din. At the other end of the chamber nobles from the Minho district were gravely discussing the skidding devaluation of the escudo. A magnificent sun was lighting the roofs of Santa Catarina, rolling along with the disorder of a stable into a transparent valley crossed by a freeway bridge. Ducks were migrating southward in triangular platoons, fleeing the bitterness of autumn. Flocks of pigeons were coming and going in a rustle of taffeta. A three-year-old prince was dragging his tin automobile along the carpet. The admiral kissed the king's hand and they both remained silent, looking at the morning-mist texture of the September afternoon.

"Forget about that penguin story," the prince said, chasing away horseflies, sweating out the liquids of an old man under the ridiculous crown. "The fact is, I missed you."

The pensioner thought how almost everything had changed in Lixbon since he'd embarked for Angola to live in the midst of the violent solitude of blacks. An epidemic of riparian ailments had practically wiped out the Tagus nymphs, reduced to a small school of graying mermaids who fed on the Chelas sewers and the sediment from the steel mills poured into the waves by means of a complicated network of canals. The people were abandoning castles and moving to Luxembourg or Germany in search of work in automobile and plastics factories. The dukes were opening bank branches in Venezuela. The officers of the Sagres school were smoking heroin cigarettes and exploring bars in Albufeira. And if the Castilians invaded the realme all they would find would be diffident Englishmen on the golf course in Estoril, sentries dropping from lack of sleep by the main gate at Army headquarters, and women dressed in black in deserted villages, spreading their skirts around wooden stools, seeing an absolute void inside themselves.

The biologists ended up leaving without the count on a frigate that disappeared from the radar screen at the latitude of

Scotland, breaking up on a perverse promontory on the same day that Vasco da Gama and the monarch, hoodwinking the bodyguards bulging with pistols that the Americans rented out by the month, sneaked out all by themselves toward Marvila, chatting about discoveries and goddesses. They'd grown so old that the people of the city, who didn't recognize them, were flabbergasted at that pair of masked old men wearing the bizarre clothing of a carnival gone by, with daggers at their waists, pointed velvet moccasins, striped jackets, and long locks smelling of pantry oregano in which parasites from other centuries proliferated. The children in Penha de França and Beato surrounded them in an uproar of amused curiosity. The women selling vegetables, startled, froze in the middle of their vending shouts. The colors of the traffic lights got all mixed up as they passed, causing a confusion of taxis, chaises, and trucks whose drivers insulted each other hatefully. They stopped for a sandwich and a beer at a lunchroom next to a gas station under the trees and over the rooftops they caught sight of anchored sailing ships and the standards of packets that the eternal gulls, the same ones that had witnessed the conquest of Lixbon by Dom Afonso Henriques, hovered over. The king and the navigator, ignoring the idlers who were mocking them, laughing at the scepter and the tin crown, walked along the Tagus toward Cabo Ruivo and the seaplane stolen from the waves and kept on its limestone promontory with pieces of cloth pulled by birds and the mummies of its passengers, behind the sentry boxes. A dozen ragamuffins were spreading shrimp nets for the crabs along the riverbank. Tagus nymphs, whose spinal hernias barely allowed them to swim, were picking barnacles off themselves near the petrochemical plant and its smell of ammoniacal guts. They ended up choosing a floating dock beyond Chelas where they were nothing but two anonymous old men decked out in an intriguing fashion and where moribund ancient ferries were being covered with moss, bird droppings, and a forgotten garret light. To the south, toward Barreiro and Alcochete, the monument to Christ the King could be seen, the steel arches of the bridge, and the opaque, lye-dull water. Behind them, in the colored irregularity of Lixbon, were the waterfront warehouses where galley commanders were idly gathering together Indian slaves, rhinoceroses, noblemen amputated by Dutch cutlasses, and barrels of triton scales, in addition to the hovels of the poor that fell apart and collapsed every year during the rainy season. Vasco da Gama and the monarch decided on an embankment alongside the river, Dom Manoel having taken off his tin crown and ermine cape and the sailor quit of the weight of his sword, and they finally sat down as equals in their decrepitude and weariness after so many separations, misunderstandings, piques, and courtiers' intrigues. The penguin frigate had crossed the harbor mouth a long time before, carrying its cargo of biologists in lab coats, incubators with ultraviolet rays, and scientific atlases, the court whispered about them for a long time in the baptismal restaurant at the São Jorge castle, the riffraff were gathering stones and boiling sunflower oil in coffeepots for the defense of the city, and we there, all alone, in the peace and quiet of the afternoon, examining the Tagus nymphs who'd lost the strength to fight against the tides, and slowly impregnating ourselves with the softness of the darkening shadows. His Majesty's old-rooster eyelids met mine, equally full of folds and wrinkles, and for a moment I was struck by the absurd idea that we were a single individual looking at himself in the mirror, surprised at the adornments around the neck, the gold earrings and buckles, squatting by the water, safe from courtiers and adulators, more vulnerable and fragile than a poor common sailor. I was getting ready to tell the king about my years in Africa, the sailing of the troops, the guerrilla fighters who came out of the interior to occupy Loanda. Talk to you about the oily belly of the bay, the clouds of white January birds, the smell of mulatto women at four in the morning, Sire, whom, once you'd experienced them, you never forgot, and the sudden miraculous dawns of the tropics. I wanted to tell him, while the Tagus nymphs evaporated, one after the other, in the blackness of the waves, about my return to Lixbon in a hold with sheets soaked in vomit and listless misery, when His Highness got up and brought over a plank from an abandoned scaffold and the bricks left over from the wall of a guard post. Two hundred yards away from us the watch was lighting the lanterns on the ships. Dom Manoel put the plank down on the bricks and wiped his hands on the satin of his thighs.

"Let's see your deck of cards," he said. "I want to see if you still know how to cheat."

At first he didn't like the Largo de Santa Bárbara because he couldn't see the ocean or hear the puppy weeping of baby walruses looking for barnacles on the reefs, but when in the morning at the time he went to bed the sun fired up the balconies of the Bairro das Colónias, Manoel de Sousa de Sepúlveda began to become accustomed to the absence of waves and to the buses and viscounts' coaches that took the place of the ships anchored in the miasma of galleys submerged in the Tagus.

At ten o'clock at night he would go into the Dona Leonor Bar (in homage to the wife under her stone angel in the land of cannibals) and from the bar direct a flock of languid girls and foul-mouthed septuagenarians whom age had inflamed as they let their arthritis climb up along thighs covered with silk stockings where a cut of meat was bursting forth. Set up on his command bridge at the bar, protected by mirrors, bottlenecks, and glasses, Manoel de Sousa de Sepúlveda falsified the cocktails by adding a third of soothing syrup or a measure of antibaldness lotion from the pharmacy next door, took the pulse of the drunkenness so as to avoid damage to the plush on the benches, regulated the intensity of the music in tune with the temperature of the clientele, and at three in the morning, when Afonso de Albuquerque or Dom Francisco de Almeida, stogies between their teeth, would spread the splendor of their beards out over the table, he would place ancient sea chanties on the turntable to soften the bitterness of the deposed viceroys. At five o'clock in the two-storied tavern on whose divans, hibernating, ground down by the suckling of their children, Mr. Francisco Xavier's mulatto women would stretch out, ships' lookouts and bank clerks would nibble at the women's ears, hidden by Formica panels, to the sound of military marches whose dying notes reached all the way to Mozambique and Japan. At five-thirty, when the first light fought with the street lamps and the viceroys, knocking over glasses, were arguing about the strategy at Trafalgar, Father António Vieira, always wearing his stole, thrown out of all the cabarets in Lixbon, would proceed to an imposing entrance, declaiming his drunken sermons until he fell onto a sofa between two black women, caterwauling the maxims of the prophet Elijah with missionary vehemence. At six o'clock the employees would gather up the little dishes of peanuts, popcorn, and banana chips, empty the ashtrays, sweep up the shells, and the customers, blinded, were suddenly awakened by the open windows of the empty discotheque while the mulatto women climbed up the hill to the Apostle of the Indies Boarding House, bumping into moonstruck policemen. On the Avenida Almirante Reis numbed stenographers waited for buses to the Baixa. A bugle woke up the cadets at the Military Academy, who rolled up their foreskins, dreaming of naked sylphs with perfect navels, wallowing on their soldier-boy sheets. The garbage trucks grazed on the trash, swaying their half-axle hips on their way to the municipal stables. A pitiless sadness faded the club's blue and white awning. Standing in the doorway in carnival overcoat and pants, surrounded by the shutters of closed shops, watching Father António Vieira blessing Arroios with papal pomp and the viceroys leaving, lurching in a precarious dance, Manoel de Sousa de Sepúlveda always had a resigned feeling of anguish comparable only to the one he'd suffered months before at Costa da Caparica leaning against the rusted shafts of the Nivea Cream ball as the waves of dawn trotted along the beach and Gypsies converged about him with their mourning figures. He felt so alone that he gave a taxi driver double the fare to drive him as fast as possible to the ground-floor apartment in Campo Pequeno where he lived, getting undressed by tearing off his clothes and remaining for hours on end lying on his back looking at the ceiling, listening in terror to the sounds of his neighbors.

He'd set up the bar and rented the apartment with a check from Belgium that had been absentmindedly stuck away in another pocket and which the cashier at the bank had held for a week, mistrustful because it had been turned in by a barefoot and half-naked character covering the freckles on his chest with the shreds of a shirt. But the next month, washed and shaved, wearing a magnificent English suit and a silk tie, he paid the grandsons of the former owner, put away in a nursing home because of an opportune thrombosis, for the transfer of the discotheque. He replaced the torn little curtains with church rose windows, installed rotating wreaths that accompanied the tangos, chose doormen and waiters from among trusted stevedores used to waterfront brawls and memorable strikes, reached an understanding with Fernão Mendes Pinto and Mr. Francisco Xavier concerning the recruitment and maintenance of a reasonable contingent of mulatto women, and he furnished the flat in Campo Pequeno with new African fossils and new cannibal assagais, ferreted out in Lixbon antiques shops. As he was never able to replace his large collection of river shells where sirens sang indistinct nostalgia in low voices, he substituted photographs of gentlemen in sideburns and ladies with fearsome eyebrows, purchased in country marketplaces with the desire to invent for himself the past he'd lost and about which, with impassioned care, he created the most superfluous details, banishing the Amoreiras Garden and his silk-merchant father and fabricating a childhood of thermal baths in Caldas da Rainha, cared for by a grandmother named Elisa, always supplied with strategic sweets and who suffered from kidney trouble. He kept only the name Manoel de Sousa de Sepúlveda (although in moments of mystic fervor he thought of changing it to Fernando de Bulhões) and the stuffed bull's head from the house of his real adolescence that his brother had ceded to him with the relief of a person getting rid of an impediment. He had to fumigate it because of the ladybugs that had nested in the nostrils and the moths that were devouring the tight skin of the jaw, and he exposed it to the sun on the rear balcony amidst wet clothes and the dishwasher in order to get rid of the last traces of the insects. He thought, in wonderment, sipping his blackberry liqueur in his easy chair in the parlor, about how he'd lived for years and years in that smell, as if he had been breathing inside the sticky coffin of a decomposing novice nun. He remembered his mother dragging her lizard ankles across the rugs between sighs, his father expelling dragonflies from his mouth, and his brother, who slept threatened by fantastic lizards, realizing that that chunk of bull acquired by a bullfighting uncle at a pawnbroker's auction was not only master of them all but of the whole house and that it spied on their most trivial actions with its provocative and stupid glass eyes. There began, then, between him and the bull on the wall, a combat that would continue on until the nobleman's death, measured by a simulated indifference, from closet to closet, watching each other rancorously from total calm, hating each other fiercely over the printed luncheon tablecloth. If he woke up to urinate, pressing the skin over his bladder with both hands, the beast would oblige him to expel through his urethra specks as sharp as hydrochloric acid, which opened their way through his flesh with an abominable drive that echoed in his insides for many hours, until, unable to bear the suffering, he gave the head, with no explanation whatever, to Father António Vieira, but was obliged to take it back eight months later by virtue of the commanding dispositions of a will along with an aborigine Christ and a print of *Guernica,* on his sentimental knees, leaning over the bed of the well-educated priest, dead from tertian ague contracted in jungles where the petals of flowers looked like the canine teeth of hyenas and rubber trees snuff out with their leaves the last vestiges of nostalgia.

Unburdened for a time of the ill-fated presence of the bull that had stopped his father from becoming rich and had kept him evening after evening clinging to the newspaper of his resignation, his prosperity grew with the inconceivable rhythm of epidemics. In a single half year he'd become the owner of bars in Areeiro, Paço da Rainha, Arroios, and on the Avenida Almirante Reis; he exploited the boardinghouses in the neighborhood, where patronesses sped up the enthusiasm of his customers by knocking on doors; he ran the taverns of dawn that help to dissipate the disbelief of daybreak; he spread out all the way to Martim Moniz, where he became partner in the shops of businessmen who fob off cheap jewelry at Christmastime to the sound of little windup bells; even the nymphs of Santa Apolónia or the Sodré Docks, who evaporate with the dawn into the gypsum of the river, paid him in doubloons twenty percent of their profits, not to mention the ones who dragged their faded low-cut gowns along the milestones of the freeways, offering truck drivers the dead pleasures of sex. He lent money to Dom João de Castro to urbanize Goa, furnished Camões with the wherewithal for a pocket edition of *The Lusiads,* with naked dancers on the cover, published in a collection of detective novels, helped the lyric poet Tomaz António Gonzaga improve his slave trade, and involved himself in the War of the Roses, taking the sides of both families in hopes of marrying, with his Linguaphone English, a redheaded duchess. And every day, at nine o'clock in the morning, after checking the cash register and gathering up the money, he would lie down with a feeling of having forgotten some obscure thing in some familiar place, as if he'd closed the door and left the bunch of keys on the inside.

In spite of his being a millionaire and a confidant of our lord the king, who would seat him next to him during the skits and farces by the goldsmith Gil Vicente, who would sometimes appear at the bar with his pockets full of notes and verses and would invariably choose the worst-dressed and ugliest chippy the patron of Setúbal had sent down that night, Manoel de Sousa de Sepúlveda, who was chairman of the board of a stock brokerage house, was piling up dollars in Switzerland, and treated Afonso de Albuquerque with great familiarity or Come on over here, Vice, where I can see your face (and the other man would get up and come over, huddling in his jacket with a submissive little look), in spite of the friendship he'd struck up during an Algarvean vacation with the Britisher, husband of a former nun in a ridiculous little bonnet, Martin Luther, he hadn't been able to buy the last discotheque he needed on the Largo de Santa Bárbara, a cave with a fan at the level of the ankles of passersby, more damp and uncomfortable than the basements of churches where vampires lay eggs in the lavender of priests' stoles, with two or three goddesses smoking in the dark and with the glow of their cigarettes calling the customers who navigated aimlessly through shadowy waters enlivened by the discordant jaws of an accordion.

The owner, a tiny man with a Lenin cap on his bald head, answered to the name of Nuno Álvares Pereira and in his youth had been Constable of the Realme and after that a Dominican friar before he grew tired of masses and Te Deums sung with his teeth chattering in a frigid nave and returned to the Order the sandals that crippled his feet and the coarse habit that gave him hives without protecting him from the cold, got his lay topcoat back, asked the Duke of Braganza, his son-in-law, for a loan, acquired the Aljubarrota Club on the corner of the Avenida Almirante Reis and the first sidestreet of the Largo, and buried himself at the table farthest from the door to observe things in darkness in the company of a watered-down capillaire, immune to his daughter's scolding, listening to the orchestra up on an oblique platform play the *cantigas de amigo* of his highness Dom Dinis.

Manoel de Sousa de Sepúlveda called on him several times in his apartment on the Rua Barão de Sabrosa with the stubborn idea, always put off, of acquiring the monk's discotheque with its feeble fan and in that way obtaining a monopoly of the waltzes and tangos of Lixbon. The former abbot lived in a concierge's quarters underneath a staircase, with a small living room with three-legged sideboards and autographed pictures of marchionesses, a diminutive bedroom watched over by the age-old eyes of a turtle, and a sink under a tin roof where centipedes and chameleons rolled about in silent combat behind the shard of a mirror. The constable, perched on a kitchen stool, with a feeble capillaire in his hand, would listen to the arguments with inexorable immobility, looking at him with his soldierly sternness as he seemed to be contemplating beyond the other man's waving hands knights in long robes galloping over a field of nettles. He'd lived too many years to put any stock in businessmen's sleight-of-hand or their maneuvers of seductive adulation, and the excessive moss on his bones was making him immune to reason and flattery and penetrable only by the love dirges of a king buried in Odivelas in the school where the daughters of military men learned by heart the names of the right-bank tributaries of European rivers along with the unsolvable mysteries of logarithmic tables. Manoel de Sousa de Sepúlveda, with no time for spying on girls' schools as in Malanje, ran up against the negative answers of the constable, who from time to time would order him to be quiet for the purpose of hearing from the strip of yard an inaudible little sound:

"Do you hear?" the soldier asked him, going for his broadsword in the dresser drawer. "It's the trumpets from the Castilian camp."

The better to persuade him, he would hang around at the Aljubarrota Club every night also with a lukewarm capillaire in his hand, putting together unanswerable and useless arguments between two weary boleros. One early morning, when the former monk spoke to him for the thousandth time about the Spanish trumpets, Manoel de Sousa de Sepúlveda, worn out by his unreasonable resistance and his senile hallucinations, gave a desperate pound on the table.

"Trumpets, shit," he roared like a man possessed. "What century do you think we're living in?"

The mulatto women, frightened, trembled under the accessories of their low-cut gowns. The dusty light coming through the ventilator was drowning out the concertina and with the clarity of day the cracked furniture, the yellow plaster, the insecure ceiling, and the sad glimmer of the paper stars could be seen. The bartender, his features deformed by several hours of gin, went out into the street in civilian clothes with the lost gait of cattle without a leader. The women went sluggishly down to the coatroom counter to get their rabbit coats. The streetlights were going out one by one, snuffed by the razor-sharp breeze of dawn, and Manoel de Sousa de Sepúlveda found himself defeated before the unbreakable military man who wouldn't bend even under the weighty tons of morning.

"I offered you a sweet deal," he told the constable, who put the capillaire down on the Formica table, stuffed the cheap stogies into his pocket. "But you don't understand a thing when it comes to money matters."

Nuno Álvares Pereira locked up the establishment and they went along together on foot toward the Campo de Santana through the deserted city, which municipal workers with rakes were clearing of trash and mulberry leaves that the breeze was scattering. The soldier, in an antique sheepskin coat, hindered by curvature of the spine, moved with difficulty, like a church biddy at mass, and in the neighborhood of Conde Redondo, where brownish forms trotted along, he tugged at the sleeve of Manoel de Sousa de Sepúlveda's expensive overcoat, made from the hair of an emir's camel.

"Can't you hear them now, the Spaniards?"

And his face was so serious and tense and his expression so determined over the disordered lump of his shoulders that Manoel de Sousa de Sepúlveda stood on the gravel, listening, trying to hear, coming from the courthouse, the clang of the invaders' armor.

f rom the mosque or French brothel luxuries of the Hotel Ritz they transferred us to a boardinghouse in Colares with a lot of flags from different countries in front and torn sheets and walls dirtied by those who'd returned from Africa before them and had wiped the green slime from their boots on the ceiling, and then to another one, two stories high, a hundred yards beyond, where milk cartons and candy wrappers were accumulating in the empty swimming pool. As they placed the wedding picture on a sideboard and the sewing machine behind the drapes, the husband felt they were living in some sort of ruins of a cataclysm or in an abandoned cemetery: the broken chandeliers hung down off the paint like heads bent in displeasure, not entirely mournful; the wood of the cabinets had been carved up with a knife; the scars on the blinds, almost reduced to their wire rods, bore witness to merciless combat with Arab ghosts; and the elevators that led directly to paradise, where Saint George, dressed as Gonçalo Mendes de Maia, was crushing his round-bellied dragon over a cloud of clay, would break down between floors groaning as if from a sprain.

From the second boardinghouse, where at night we inhaled the pregnant-bitch smell of the sea, seen in the distance above the eucalyptus trees in the shape of a dark fog that blended with the sky and where the large ships of the dead danced weightlessly, they moved us, along with twenty-odd other families, to an unoccupied house in Ericeira that faced the escarpment by the ocean where the dampness condensed into little birds the color of water that the waves spat out from crag to crag. The house must have belonged to a colonel because it smelled strongly of a mess hall and when the woman hid the sewing machine under the couch she came across some infantry leggings, without buckles now, gathering a crust of mildew, and some radish stems on the floor. A gentleman with his hair parted in the middle and a small trimmed mustache, right out of a turn-of-the-century fashion magazine, gathered them together casually into rooms that were at the top of an irregular tower with balconies overlooking the cliffs, the night, and the mouth of the Lisandro, he had them served coffee in the morning and soup at nightfall, and he disappeared forever on the road to Lixbon on board a jeep driven by a sailor more earthbound than a mole, who'd deserted a long time ago or had never experienced the trade winds of adventure.

At that time of year, almost October, there were still a half dozen vacationers in Ericeira and a few awnings on the frigid beach in front of the alleys with chalets that were like ancient urinals, invaded by virgin vines and scorpions. The wind carried along the bells from Mafra, which sounded like the remote gaze of evaporated ancestors. Autumn and the ash gray of its smoke made them feel that they were in an almost deserted village with a few cabin boys on the narrow sidewalks, trawlers that never went out to sea, and people as old as they in the yard of an empty church with carved saints leaning over in gloomy threats. The cold was rusting the needles on the sewing machine that wasn't in operation in spite of the wife's habit of pulling the buttons off all shirts and all jackets; simply to sew them on again. The promise of rain disjointed the cornices of the roofs. The trees stood out on the square, casually tossing about their quartered members of four or five panic-stricken branches. The morning coffee had the taste of the mud that climbed up through the crumbled grating of the bidets in time to the sighing of the water. The nuptial portrait was a completely indistinguishable blotch by now, bereft of any detail except the imagined smile of the woman who was blushing with embarrassment and surprise. The husband remembered the last time he'd heard her voice, in Bissau, saying After fifty-three years in Africa I don't belong here anymore, and how they'd completely lost the habit of talking, carrying on a dialogue with each other through the medium of a schematic alphabet of evasive gestures, and he decided to invite her, in spite of her age, to start life clean, from the beginning, somewhere in the world.

"Even the North Pole," he argued, "it certainly must be better than this."

But his wife, centuries ago, had passed over the gloomy border of hope, where even the most trivial of plans were looked upon with unshakable indifference. The old man was faced with the impression that his wife was living in the little house of her childhood in Barcelos once more, strangled by the odor of the medlar trees. She was seven or eight years old, wore light little dresses, and was learning to play the cello in the afternoon with an old maid who kept waving her fan to drive away the heat of her virginity. He shuddered at the idea of finding himself married to a student of solfeggio and he was even more upset when she would answer him ceremoniously in a voice full of the romantic consonants of an antiquated orthography:

"Please to leave me, sir, as I must needs practice a toccata."

Incapable of enduring the absurd position of being his own wife's great-uncle, he tried to jog her memory with reminiscences of Bissau, the death of their daughter, the long deep fogs, the lady on the floor below going after gnats with the heel of her shoe, the inaugural performance at the Cine-Theatro with a company from Coimbra putting on *The Lady of the Camellias* for an audience receptive to the bleats of love, saturated with sweat and emotion. But his wife, who'd loosened her bun and tied organdy bows onto her gray locks, listened to him without hearing, moving her fingers to the ternary rhythm of the music, wrapped in cocoon of keys with no opening. Turned toward the windows on the sea that was rolling up the leaves of its waves onto the beach in front with the first rains, she was waiting with motionless anxiety for the arrival of the music teacher, dead for almost ten decades, or on the bed or under the blanket she looked for the invisible instrument whose echoes seemed to reverberate in the rooms during the pauses in bronchitis. After a month of arguments, begging, explanations, and discourses, he left her alone, wrinkled and tiny like an aged child, sketching on the beveled mirror with the tip of her finger a confusion of chords, boarded the van to Lixbon at the square with humble shops and rustic winter buildings, sat down beside a man who reeked of goat cheese, and for three hours went through nameless hamlets, misty forests, shortcuts ruined by potholes, the burial of a count fallen into disgrace in the eyes of the king, all alone in a rented hearse and with a village band behind blowing flutes that melancholy muted, until I got to the capital again, not to the shoreline as when returning from Guinea, but by the workshops and factories on the inland side, sad in the painful sorrow of January until the man who smelled of goat cheese, sleeping with his chin on his chest, declared in his dreams, under his beret, Tomorrow I'm going to have an X ray at the Institute, the small palms by taverns disappeared, the avenues divided and multiplied in neighborhoods where he'd never been, and the husband realized that he'd really arrived in Lixbon from the incalculable number of convents and clandestine city blocks, and also by the seraphim who took shelter on the knees of statues, just like doves, smoothing their wet wings with celestial lips.

For the first few months he stayed in Benfica in a group of structures made out of rubble in the shelter of the cemetery wall and which were occupied by filthy Cape Verdeans quick with a switchblade, who drove hammers in street repairs and had the sweet putrefaction smell of gravediggers in common with distant relatives with blankets over their knees whom they would visit at Christmastime in anticipation of condolences. At night oil lamps floated over the surface of alleys, children and dogs mingled the despair of their weeping, and the black men from the garbage trucks would cram together in what passed for a tavern, where a lame girl with wild kinky hair served bottles of tangerine liquor from a bar built from the cabin closet of a lugger that had run aground in Caxias by the prison block where the police rarefied the air with their unhealthy belches.

The old man, who'd found employment as an unemployed person and who would stand in line periodically before dawn with his colleagues in the profession to receive his laborious check at a window more distant than Russia where an impatient bureaucrat was muttering to himself the frustrations of a Phoenician usurer, send half of the amount to Ericeira meant to pay for the lessons with the invisible teacher who'd plunged his wife into an abyss of infancy punctuated with adagios, and keep what was left for the frizzy-headed girl's liquor, whose fruit alcohol, after the tenth glass, brought him back to the memory of his mother peeling arbutus berries on the bench in the yard. He was too old now to go with the forty-year-old vagrant women who would visit the bar, slippered and funereal, to impose the dew of their groins on men too drunk to be interested in their chimerical services, and it hurt him not to be able to go along with them on disjointed mattresses, witnessing, through holes in the roof, with marveling shock, the progressive dissolution of the night. He contented himself with spying on them from a distance through the valerian smell of the blacks, remembering the time when he entered a rented room, his teeth chattering with fear, led by a woman's laugh, and the surprise with which he felt himself die over the foam of two breasts, tormented by the frustration of desire and the reluctance to consult the pharmacist when he saw the burning of shameful sicknesses dripping onto his pants. When the lame girl, sick of tangerines, would shoo the last blacks into the street of excited owls and moving shadows, he would take ceremonious leave of the forty-year-olds, kissing the flea-market rings on their fingers in accordance with what as a young man he'd seen dukes do to the queen's ladies-in-waiting, coming out of the movies or from services at the cathedral, and he would doze off on the sheets with his eyes open, stroking the naked stomachs that peopled the rainy dawns with the most secret of fingers. Every Sunday he made plans to go off to Ericeira to attend a cello lesson, but the joints calcinated by age stopped him from moving, paralyzed in a jacket that was too big for his incurable thinness, and he would stay in the neighborhood, stretched out on his sheet, attending winter and the mallow-colored clouds on a trip to the sea in the shape of lyrical packets with no rest possible, lunching on a package of crackers skewered into the hole of his navel. His only adventure consisted of moving to a small room in Cruz Quebrada, above the foam of the sea and the absence of gulls, which were devouring one another at the railroad station with intemperate passion. Now, during the breaks in his laborious profession of unemployment, which obliged him constantly to fill out forms in quintuplicate, all with the proper signature, coming and going from office to office and from ministry to ministry, with useless papers, undergoing interminable interrogations by psychologists who wanted him to draw trees and decipher ink blots, subjecting himself to stethoscopes, electrocardiograms, machines that measured his blood pressure, with useless doctors and eye charts on the wall, turning in photocopies attesting to good moral and civic behavior destined for the wastebaskets of functionaries with zealous dandruff, and finally receiving the little piece of paper with his salary after fourteen hours of uninterrupted waiting, blowing on the icy flowers of his hands in front of the bank window he would relax by joining in from the windowsill the tranquillity of fishermen along the Marginal, who, creel beside them, soaked from the sprinkle of the wind and by the waves that leaped up the wall, bedecked in oilskin capes and hoods, pulled in insignificant little fish with the bend of their rods.

Around that time he got a letter from his wife in Ericeira with the news that the music lessons had ended because of the departure of the old-maid teacher, invited by Mozart himself to help with the orchestration of his *Requiem*. The pupil, enriched by supplementary notions of sight-reading, found herself with the tremendous desire to begin a concert career in New York immediately: they saw each other for a few minutes in the waiting room at the airport and the old man found a wife in a flared skirt, knit socks, and bangs, hunched over the instrument

case and with her mind made up to be a star in America with
her sublime talent. In her luggage she was carrying the sewing
machine from Guinea, with the help of which she was prepared
to turn out, during intermissions in the concerts, shawls and
robes from pieces of the stage curtain. They stood facing each
other, not talking, alien to the trooping of passengers and the
Moroccan-market hubbub of the duty-free shop, and the husband, hemmed in by Germans and baggage carts, stared at her,
trying to remember the days of their courtship, of which there
remained only the memory of a serious girl with an elusive
waist, straight as a walnut chair. The sweetheart he'd loved,
however, had vanished with the final disappearance of the
betrothed couple in the picture, shrouded by the years in the
metal case. Even the long death agony of their daughter was a
nonexistent memory buried by so many events and later misfortunes, so without any feeling of loss he witnessed the embar-
kation of a woman who gave the intriguing impression that she'd
never been his: an unknown and adolescent old woman with a
Bakelite brooch of cherries on her lapel on her way to the United
States with the cello on her back and sketching out in the void
with the thread of her arm, alien to him and the disorder of the
airport, the third movement of Mahler's *Fifth Symphony*. He
watched her go through the police gate, passport control, the
characters who look for Palestinian terrorists' machine guns in
the fuzz of teddy bears, and finally climb aboard, without a good-
bye wave, clutching the instrument to her belly, a codfishing
vessel that was filling out its sails in the direction of Broadway.

He went back to Cruz Quebrada, dazzled by the lights, by
the noise, by the absurd dialects of the turbaned Hindus who
were waiting as they dined on shards of glass for the flight from

Karachi, he grabbed the photograph of the newlyweds in which, with great effort, he could make out a bit of ribbon and the corner of a veil, and he threw it off the balcony onto the garbage heap in the rear. Without a past suddenly, ripened in the contemplation of the fishermen on the wall and their hooks of unimaginable persistence, with the idea that sooner or later a Tagus nymph, off course because of the February currents, would take the line and one of the men in an oilskin hat would dump into his creel on top of a nest of eels one of the disappointed fortyish women from the tangerine-liquor bar, a Sevillean hook dug into one side of her painted locks.

iogo Cão saw them for the first time when our
lord the king ordered that regular traffic of ves-
sels be established between Portugal and Amsterdam in order to pour into Europe the filigree of
goldsmiths and the cinnamon from the Indies, and with the
arrival of all the ships, safe and sound, we came upon a city of
lens-grinding philosophers who went along the streets on anachronistic bicycles. We saw Argentinean frigates and Turkish cruisers dozing in port, little old ladies who were startled by our
muskets, our linen adornments, and the fact that we ate with
our fingers, and at night, strolling through the city, the discoverer found himself on an avenue paved with fluorescent penta-
gons and the reflection of canals, with door upon door of gin
bars and lighted windows displaying women with red garters
sprawled on easy chairs and waving shark bones at him. So he
stopped in front of a tall, fat woman with bare breasts, a forgotten cigar in her lipsticked lips, and he thought, slapping his brow
like someone who suddenly remembers something, Hell, now
I understand why our rivers are deserted, the nymphs have mi-
grated to this place in a flock.

The ossified encyclical arguments of the chaplain about the
impenetrability of God's judgments became necessary in order
to convince him not to take two or three of the strongest and
fleshiest on board with the intention of repopulating Caxias with
painted eyes and sheer panties, because every night, immediately
after dining on water and dried meat, he would go back to the

avenue with show windows in great wonderment, stroking his ancient mariner's beard with his thumb, almost run down by the bicycles with tiny rear wheels that spun about in an atmosphere of gin, and the night before his return he got so close to the throne of an ageless queen bee with solemn thighs, lying belly-up on silk cushions that the woman ended up spotting the great-grandfather with a dagger in a carnival masquerade among the crowd of tourists, invited him in through a side door, and as I went up the two steps I came upon you, love of my soul, busy trying unsuccessfully to close the drapes of the show window and offering me the planispheric breadth of your buttocks. I had to help her unfasten a couple of rings hooked together and that was how we came across him out here on the promenade, perched up on a stool in a whore's bedroom, solving upholstery problems, and we were so ashamed that we withdrew a few steps into the shadow of the trees by the canal with the dream that no one would suppose that we were the subordinates, just imagine, of an idiot consumed by ridiculous ecstasies, on all fours, kissing the ass of a slut, barely hidden by a row of curtains, hugging her ankles, rubbing his chin over her misshapen teats, a whore who was slimier than the hunchbacked monsters who offer themselves in the Leiria area to the uncritical hunger of truck drivers or the seventy-year-old women with thinning hair and a thirst for perverted schoolboys, and that was how we saw him, getting undressed with sighs in an explosion of hooks and clasps, seams and buttons, in an urgent drive until he finally ran aground, kicking victoriously, on a torso that continued smoking behind the glass panel, indifferent to the groans of my exhalation, which tore the pillows and raised up a cloud of feathers in the darkness as if all the doves in the world were moaning with me in the last shudder of my kidneys.

The following morning, when we were fitting out the fleet, Diogo Cão appeared on the dock with purple rings under his eyes, staggering from fatigue, dragging the gigantic creature along by the hand, both dressed as if for a baptism or a burial, accompanied by two suitcases with labels from Paris hotels, a gramophone with a horn speaker, a stack of records, and a lady's bicycle, and he asked the chaplain to marry them right there because he'd found happiness, Father, you can't imagine the stormy smell of her armpits, the unbelievable taste of a waning moon on her neck, the roar of a flood in her unmotivated loud laughter, the skill these foreign chicks have in drinking up our souls with a kiss, if we stayed here another day not even your eminence, I swear, would be able to stand it, you'd experience a paradise more celestial than all the jubilees in the world, but the chaplain, alert to the wiles of the devil, kept his apostolic firmness in the face of the requests, the commands, the threats of being hanged from the mainmast, countering him with the intransigence of the prophets and the unyielding virtue of the saints. We watched them face to face from up above as we unfurled the sails, arguing on the dock at the same time that the gabby woman, disgusted with them, flirted with Hungarian lookouts and colossal stevedores tattooed with anchors, compasses, and birds, and with the passage of hours of very complicated negotiations, acts of mutual concession, and reciprocal advances, just when the commander and the servant of God, reaching some obscure understanding, embraced each other emotionally, mingling mustaches and tears, and turned to the lady from the avenue of show windows with the idea of escorting her solemnly on board, all they found were the bags, the stack of records, the abandoned gramophone, and the distant Dutch

Tagus nymph pedaling along at the opposite end of the water-front in pursuit of a Rembrandt with a goatee on his chin and a broad-brimmed hat across the surface of the dikes.

Back in Lixbon, after almost perishing off the Galician coast when American pirates with knives between their teeth, eye patches, and parrots perched on shoulders attempted an ostentatious boarding right out of a neighborhood movie house, with Errol Flynn leading them in obeyance to Cecil B. DeMille's megaphone, Diogo Cão, deaf to the king's summonses, busied himself in an unsuccessful search in the most unlikely neighborhoods for the miracle of a whore showcase capable of transporting him to the canals of Amsterdam and to the women with red garters sitting on silk pillows or in harem chairs. He lost himself in inquiries at doors that didn't open in the putrid blocks of Madragoa about blond goddesses enthroned on pillows embroidered with glass beads, and all he encountered were jellyfish drifting on the corners, floating in the ebb-tide vomit of Turkish first mates. He sought her in the clarity of Alcântara at six o'clock on August afternoons when the transparency of the air makes things so diaphanous that flocks of buildings with blue tiling flutter over the bridge like turtledoves, flapping the clothes hanging from their wings up and down, and he found a peddler hawking to no one in particular a syrup that was infallible against the evil eye and a dozen cats pining away from their voracious sexual drive on the dunghill of an empty fountain. He pursued her in the morning in the thousand bewildering blind alleys of Ajuda that don't lead anywhere except to themselves by means of an inextricable maze of small stairs, and he stumbled onto a blindman with visionary eyebrows, supplied with a table of paper model mills for children at so many escudos the dozen.

He thought he saw her, finally, in the clandestine buildings on the outskirts of the city inhabited by department-store clerks, street photographers, and secretaries overcome by irretrievable ugliness, and he sank down into construction-material debris and abandoned machinery with asparagus and lilies flourishing in the wheels, and he would have gone on looking for her, resting up from my search from tavern to tavern, calling up to every balcony in the incessant colorless wailing of beggars, if His Majesty, angry with my wine bills, with all those chalk marks on the barrels, unworthy, he said of an admiral of the realm, hadn't withdrawn my pay, deprived me of my titles and duties, and forbidden me from looking for you in the alleyways of Lixbon so I could tear your satins once more with the urgency of my fingernails, because it pained the soul of people to find him drunk and asleep on the benches of the Rossio or rolling on the sidewalk, making speeches to the sparrows. Orders had been given to the police to lead him, with great excuses, to São José Hospital, This way, admiral sir, please be so kind and don't give us a hard time, we've got your ladyfriend waiting for you at the airport, the doctors would give him an injection, the orderlies shaved his head and deloused him, he was furnished with some decent clothing and the argument Put this nice suit on, it's the latest style in Amsterdam, and, unwillingly, having heard the Council of State and consulted the political parties for parliamentary approval, I sent him to Angola, where they didn't know him, with a discreet little job as inspector for the Water Company, or, that is, in lucid moments he would check on one or two of the meters and soon they no longer pestered him, didn't ask for any report, limited themselves to giving him his stipend with my personal advice to forget about him, a man

who'd sailed like few others until the fever of the Tagus nymphs
and the mania for the sirens of Cacilhas twisted the machinery
of his judgment. They put him on an airplane with colonists
after giving him their solemn assurance that Loanda was full of
aquatic teats, Go ahead and carry all this out and send me a
detailed report with percentages and graphs to the Ministry
of Fisheries and the Directory of Cultural Heritage, because,
naturally, everybody approves of our repopulating the river
with those little creatures, well, now, take care of the matter
for me, leave the rest to me and when you leave close the door
as it should be, there's a devilish draft, have the chancellor show
Mr. Ferdinand Magellan in, what does that pest want now?

Diogo Cão lived in Loanda for twelve years, seven months,
and twenty-nine days, always in a little house in the Alvalade
district that the tropical wisteria and lizards of Africa kept erod-
ing, rolling into the garden the empty bottles of fake gin bought
on the sly from radiomen on Sicilian freighters who checked the
watermarks on the banknotes by holding them up to the bulb
in their cabin, but he would linger most of the time in the Ilha
cabarets among the medics on leave from the war who had fun
with his maps of a purported seaman, filled him with the disin-
fectant smell of their tables, and got him drunk on palm wine
in order to hear him tell about trips throughout the world, a
few sad tales invented by an old clown who fell asleep drooling
in the middle of his stories and would wake up roaring Spanish
galleons to the port side, break out full sail to the wind. The
musicians in the orchestra laughed at him, the waiters in green
jackets and bow ties laughed at him, the striptease dancers
laughed at him, whispering into the ears of their rich customers, and I, who was the oldest of all of them, the one nobody

ever chose because I looked like a sea lion with a goiter, decorating the bar as I examined my strawberry-blond locks in the mirror behind the necks of the bottles, ended up at six in the morning taking that shameful remnant of an admiral, almost drowning in his own phlegm, smelling of the absence of soap and the incontinent urine of senile drunks, with me, I helped him along, bearing up under his hippopotamus snoring and the dried-mussel stench of his skin, all the way to my shack on the beach under the palms, forty feet from the sea. He laid his sailor's perpetual restlessness down on the earthen floor of the room and when I woke up, called by the voices of my colleagues in huts near mine, I discovered him barefoot, squatting by the edge of the sea, more lucid and attentive than an astronomer, looking at the almost motionless broth of the waves for the mad certainty of a nymph.

For twelve years, seven months, and twenty-nine days Diogo Cão sought them zealously, by royal decree, in the very places where they should be sought, that is, in cabarets at night and on the beach in the morning: one by one he plumbed the shacks of Ilha, pushing aside cloths, stumbling over children's chamber pots and indignant chickens; he probed the weeds along the bank with his sword in search of sirens' triangular eggs; he ordered fishermen to stop their rowboats so he could inspect the seaweed, the snakes, and the dead gulls in their nets, but he would end up rotting away every dawn with longing for Holland, breathing in the vapors on my mat, a commander without a ship who would go into the city, ring any doorbell, ask from the doormat about the water meter and go down the steps without waiting for an answer in his haste to scrutinize from the calm of my hut the ebb tide of sunset: Do you want to bet that a minute won't go by before I catch one? he would challenge me, It's only a minute from Amsterdam to Loanda swimming. At dusk he'd help quiet my neighbors' small children by singing chanties of a calm sea or delighting them with endless tales of funerals on board; he'd repair their toy windup cars and on the day he collected his pay he'd give them dolls with straw eyelashes that sobbed their name in the slow voice of an oracle. I was beginning to feel less lonely and happier, sweetening the secret plans of an old love affair with the Tagus-nymph civil servant who talked to me all the time about lens grinders pedaling through a mist of canals until they shipped out most of the girls to Europe on big ships full of women and forgot about me because my body wasn't the right age for boardinghouses in Lixbon. The blacks took over all of this, set up Yugoslavian machine-gun nests in the arcades, murdered one another with cannon fire, and came and went into the jungle and back, driven on by bloody acts of vengeance. The harbor filled with canoes and galleys destined to bring the bitterness of the colonists home, the huts on the island emptied out, and one morning I didn't find the admiral observing the soup of the waves with his usual lookout's concentration, just as I didn't come across him among the corpses piled up in the morgue or the ones decomposing freely on the pavement. Concerned, I went to check at the Water Company and they sent me from the Dripping Faucets window to the Disappeared and Deceased Section, where a skinny mulatto who called me comrade and was cleaning his fingernails with a toothpick thumbed through a file, thumbed through a register, thumbed through a notebook with grocery bills, got lost in the learned contemplation of a folding map, swore that he would send an answer through proper channels to the window of Socialist Replanning on the fourth floor just past the small window for Broken Pipes, and after three weeks of contradictory wanderings from line to line, where they gave me a negative answer or affirmed or had affirmed what they had denied, they finally showed me, with an expression of pity, a kind of list with lots of names and dates and ID numbers of state employees, and they told me, pointing with the tip of a ballpoint, Here he is, take a good look, see, it's been more than a month since that bird took the plane to Lixbon, so when I got home I didn't even go in, I lay down in the shade of a palm tree and I went over to the edge of the water, limping because of the tight shoes, not thinking about anything, not feeling anything, not imagining anything, looking for the sylphs that float along among the hulls of ships.

The man named Luís was still writing octaves over the same mineral water on the esplanade of the café at Santa Apolónia station, occasionally pointing his empty eye, which seemed to see backward, toward baggage handlers with their little duck steps under huge trunks or toward drug dealers who were scratching their backs in the neighborhood of the newsstand, when the waiter with the ballpoint took up his shift again and outfitted himself in the pantry with his yellow buttons. The skylight in the ceiling was turning to night, first dusty and pink, like the course of love, the color of the river outside, and then completely dark, with an absolute blackness peopled with the sparse and imprecise lights of invented ships that were like drifting, spectral aircraft. The limited from Madrid arrived with scorching steam, snorting scalding water out its snout, and a freight train started up on the last set of tracks with endless laziness, the horns of Minho oxen and the noses of mules showing through the slats in the cars. The green roof lights of taxis marked off the darkness again as they waited with engines running and the unbelievable patience of spiders. The magazines at the newsstand, under the title "Golf Is My Only Passion," featured exclusive interviews with Afonso de Albuquerque, sitting by his fireside, Doberman at his feet, in his home in Estoril. The waiter, napkin over his arm now, cleaned one or two barrelheads, moved chairs, ordered an invisible slave hidden by the wall of yogurt containers and soft drinks at the counter Bring out a cup of tea and a rice cake right away, he sniffed, as he passed by the man named Luís, interested in the cardboard package where the remains of his father smelled of clothes-bin yeast, and he disappeared into the midst of hatbands, cigarette lighters, and American tobacco, summoned by a finger in the air.

But night still hadn't found the precise spot on which to locate its mysterious objects of shadows and fluorescent tubes, the fearsome darkness and the artificial sun of metallic bulbs, and it was seeking itself out nervously, blinking its light on the cement of the floor. So bootblacks took advantage to attack ankles that withdrew out of fear, the nine o'clock beggars here and there in topcoats that flapped over their long johns, snaring with spry fingers the crushed butts on the platform, characters with mistrustful faces going from Intendente to Alfama, stopping at the station for a dinner of fritters, pursued by informers and police. At eleven o'clock, when the beer froth on the Tagus reached eye level and what was left of the old man's body underwent a cataclysm of shuddering before settling down in the sawdust of the box, the waiter halted in front of him, balancing a tray of capillaires on the palm of his hand and asking me over the grease decorations of his jacket without even a glance of interest at my poem Isn't that my pen? and I said yes without interrupting the rhymes, because the idea of a reasonable image had come to me, and for half an hour or so I had him at my table, complaining about what a bitchy life it was, we earn a pittance, you know, everything goes to taxes and fees, a bitter fellow, middle-aged, a radio ham who lived in the Bairro Alto with his wife, five descendants, and his invalid father-in-law on a couch in front of an altar of idols with a blanket on his knees, You can't even dream of what fate has done to me, and just when

I was about to answer, angry at having my epic disturbed, because we all have our troubles, what the hell, me, for example, I can't get rid of my father whom I'm carrying here, and his bones, or what was left of his bones, squeaked softly, startling the other man, whose name was Garcia da Orta, pleased to meet you, he grew medicinal plants on his balcony, he'd been born in Manteigas, and he drew back in fright (Are you kidding me or what?) staring in terror at the old man's femurs.

The woman in the apron at the newsstand locked it up and went off, the beggars were sleeping in the waiting room with pillows of newspapers folded under their heads; the lamps on the ships quivered on the water, and I put the ballpoint and the octaves in my pocket and explained to the waiter about the killings in Loanda, the deceased laid out on the dining room table, the coffin in Alcântara, the customs guard with his musket, reassuring him I had him touch the sawdust packing and the dead man's liquid, and the radio ham, calmer now, suggested to me Instead of burying him why don't you sell him to me for fertilizer, I've started an experiment at home with laxatives in flowerpots in my father-in-law's room, on Saturdays I pour a spoonful of ground thallus down his gullet, but nothing so far, just little balls of goat shit on the sheet and it's a drag, I won't rest until the bastard empties out his gut.

At the end of Garcia da Orta's shift, at seven o'clock in the morning, when night sailed slowly off to darken some other country, he took me to the back of the pantry, where he hung up the jacket with buttons and lumps and changed into one of fake crocodile skin, the kind that shrinks to half its size with the second washing, we opened the cardboard box and its guano atmosphere, pushed the sawdust back, and the same as in pharmacies, we poured my father, using the blade of a fish knife, into a milk bottle, cartilages, tendons, joints, watery little pieces of flesh, the false teeth were in good shape and I put them in my pants pocket for when I'd be just as old and cheekless as he was, condemned to sucking on chicken bones like a disappointed faggot. When, bottle under my arm, we reached the square, or what I thought was a square, in front of the train station, all I could see was a dampness of gulls, Castilian spies under trucks beside the river, and dozens of Fernando Pessoas, very serious, with glasses and mustaches, on the way to their jobs as bookkeepers in Pombaline buildings with ceramic eaves gnawed at by the cancer of dry rot and varnished cockroaches that were like wedding shoes with antennae.

Garcia da Orta lived on the top floor of a three-story building on the Rua do Norte, with a grocery store on the ground floor and a morning bustle of neighbors and dogs from the square with the statue. The sea was visible between intervals of doves, dice games in furtive alleys, melancholy newspaper offices, and fado houses transformed into remnant stores. We went up the stairs, running into the dew of dinners from the night before on seamstress landings until we came upon a creature in a bathrobe with a dozen children around her, a tremendous radio crackling with distant voices, and an old man sleeping on a shredded pillow besieged by boxes of flowers that were strangling him with slow vegetable craftiness and took up the whole apartment, driving the furniture, the children, and the gas meter out the window into the hawking sounds of the street.

It was hard for us to move in the thick atmosphere of aromatic leaves destined to cure constipation, elephantiasis, male sterility, catalepsy, varicose veins, and crossed eyes. At the table a hairy tentacle with a guaranteed effect on the measles was always waiting for a forkful of luncheon potatoes; red stamens sucked up the sauce from the meat with an aspirating little whistle; the carnivorous tulips for infusions against sinusitis were tied to their pots so they wouldn't swallow people. From time to time a mournful whispering, coming from Canada or Macau, would buzz on the radio, Come in P34, come in P34, JS90 here, I'm listening, over, and Garcia da Orta would immediately abandon his explanation of the cultivation of a special grain destined to wipe out the martyrdom of bunions, would arm himself with a cutlass and a visored helmet, and take off in the direction of the apparatus, slicing through a forest of tendrils that cleansed the skin of boils, liver spots, and various itches. We put down our spoons, interrupted our soup in sorrow, some of the children wept, clutching their mother, who was waving good-bye toward the curative grove with her handkerchief, and for hours on end we would listen, relieved, to a series of discordant electrical capers and the roars of the radio ham who had survived and was proclaiming with conviction P34 here, P34 here, I'm listening, over.

The man named Luís got a bed on the Rua do Norte in return for the milk bottle with his father's corpse, and in a short time he got used not only to sleeping on the level of the kitchen bricks, up against the stove, where the medicinal plants were satisfied during hungry urges to sink their gnashing teeth, polyps, and roots into the garbage cans, but also to strangers conversing in code from Korea or Bulgaria with the capillaires waiter from the train station about the new carburetors on automobiles from Tokyo or the annual performance of the People's Ballet of Sofia. In the morning the wife would clap her hands

to drive off the intruding bushes that hindered her from cooking by taking over the water for the rice, a vine would pick up a
child at random and disappear into some spongy foliage, and
the man named Luís, after watering the pots with a pinch of
father, would go out into the neighborhood to witness the
murderous arguments of the women fishmongers, their enormous gullets reverberating with fury, to admire the proud car-
riage of the Gypsies who pulled their carts of blatant poverty
behind them along the cobblestones of the street, or to watch
from the top of the Rua do Alecrim the Sodré Docks and the
rocking of the caravels down below. He continued the poem in
a peaceful little pastry shop on Príncipe Real, where bald-headed
widowers impregnated with chaste nostalgia sucked in the tea
for perpetual constipation with tiny sips while I, unmindful of
their coughs and the persistence of the blowflies on the bean
cakes, would write about tempests and councils of gods with a
martini glass within reach of my beard.

As I neared the Rua do Norte on my way back home, right
away, on the square with my statue in the center and despite
the machinery in blacksmith shops, the polishing snap of bootblacks, and the hammers of carpenters, I would hear the moon-
quake of the wisterias that were infallible for difficult digestion
as they struggled gluttonously against the planks of the balconies after the pigeon eggs forgotten on the roof tiles, and immediately thereupon Garcia da Orta, celebrating with howls his
hopes for improvement from chicken pox on the part of a Polish radio ham, reduced by the distance to half a dozen strange
stammers. The botanist's wife served a boiled dinner, half-
devoured by violets specialized for uterine prolapse and impacted
wisdom teeth, and she would huddle at a corner of the table,

afraid of the spinach for bad breath and the geraniums for anklosis, and while she peeled fruit for the surviving children, who had escaped the hunger of the plants, she would answer the paralytic, who spoke to her from the next room about winter in Manteigas, about the snow crystals that sparkled on the eyelids of the dead in spite of the crèche atmosphere of wakes, of wolves with nightmare eyes who trotted through the village, who spoke to her about the murmur of wine in the pines and the volcanic stench of animals in the stable underneath the bedroom, who spoke to her of the past, damn it, of the past, who demanded his socks and his undershirt so he could check the damage to the tomato plants from the frost, Alzira, just because of the simple desire to see the sea I accepted moving to Lixbon and marrying a madman with his wireless and his seeds, and the sea is nothing but a fishbowl there with all the ships coming back from Africa, loaded with penniless colonists, crazy people who sell their father's ashes like that idiot we're taking care of there who doesn't even have good manners, smearing fat all over himself when he eats, every so often declaiming phrases that nobody understands written down on an order pad, the sea, damn it, the stinking sea and this city that smells like a toilet and a dump, Never mind, Papa, never mind, she shouted at the old man, deaf to a Hungarian dialogue on the radio, this summer at the latest we're going to the mountains.

She didn't get to go nor did she even have to do a lot of hollering or prepare any bunches of onions for the trip because a week before their departure a clump of begonias swallowed the paralytic in one gulp at siesta time while a domesticated petunia was clipping the children's nails. The man named Luís was writing about the disastrous loves of ladies-in-waiting and

kings on the luncheon oilcloth and Garcia da Orta was com-
municating through his buttons with a Persian religious leader
converted to Hertzian waves by his fifteenth concubine, the
godchild of the Mexican consul, with whom he exchanged im-
pressions of brothels and vague scientific notions out of a high
school textbook. The botanist's wife, who happened to be passing with the clothes basket under her arm by the door to the
paralytic's cubicle, could still make out a corola ruminating on
a checkered slipper and immediately thereafter the pleasant di-
gestive calm of the plants surrounding the empty chair in the
sea of which the memory of the dead man's buttocks was engraved. Garcia da Orta, torn from his dialogue of grunts and
sighing mechanisms with the man in a turban, threatened the
flowers, wagging his finger, saying he would grind them up into
tea for rheumatism, and he ended up putting on mourning
clothes and organizing a paranoiac ceremony around a coffin
full of stalks that he sprinkled with a watering can to the consternation of the neighbors. The men from the funeral parlor,
professionals in sadness with tape measures in hand, refused to
hold a burial for a flowerpot in a hearse with candles and the
doctor they'd brought to make out the death certificate could
only perceive as he applied his stethoscope to the roots the tiny
tearful sound of the melting snow and the rustling of eucalyptus branches at eleven o'clock in the morning in Manteigas. So
they ended up keeping the paralytic at home, completely dissolved in the medicine for otitis until a hedge of sunflowers for
a stiff neck and fractured ribs submerged the memory and the
daughter took a trip to see an aunt in Pinhel, with plane trees
and the country houses of émigrés slipping past the window, a

lunch bowl in her lap wrapped in the shirt the dead man had never worn.

During the orphan's stay in the north as she wandered in Beira through the debris of winter Garcia da Orta and the man named Luís, not to mention the children, who were disappearing one by one partaken of by wolf's bane and nard (a bougainvillea stalk took care of the last one with a single bulldog bite), underwent the wandering hunger of the abandoned, looking for crumbs in cupboards, licking cold grease from plates, and scrounging in the bag behind the door for bread crumbs, ending up by going out occasionally for a meal of soup and vegetables in a cheap bar in spite of the urgent appeals from Eskimos crackling on the radio and the medicinal Amazonia of the apartment as it continued to grow at a delirious pace and prevented their return by means of a barrier of poppies gnashing their monstrous teeth on the landing.

They continued on to the Rua do Loreto, peeping into workers' restaurants where the burned oil from fried food floated in the air like must in an attic. They deciphered the price of fish in the spelling mistakes on menus stuck on windows. They lingered in lunchrooms over red wine so thick it could be eaten with a spoon. They went into ecstasies at a snack bar with superb ice cream, organ pipes stuffed with blisters, and roast suckling pigs with piñon nuts in their ears, laid out on a bed of thyme and parsley, but they ended up dining on a timid drink of rotgut in a grocery store that was still open, with an aged gentleman enjoying the coolness by the door, ensconced on a potato barrel and fanning himself with the breeze of the electoral predictions in the evening paper, while at that moment on the top floor on the Rua do Norte the plants for diabetes were taking over the apartment and starting to advance down the stairs with an aim to seizing the basset hound and mask collection of the neighbor below, a department-store cashier, always attended by redheaded boys in tight pants and dark glasses who resembled the oil paintings of princes in the caves of Altamira at the Museum of Ancient Art. They nursed successive glasses of liquor while the pensioner with the fan dragged himself off, newspaper under his arm, to a nearby ground-floor apartment with peepholes veiled by polka dot curtains. The owner of the grocery store had to send them away at eleven-thirty, protesting God what a night I've had, Jesus, and the two of them sat down on the doorstep to chat in the voices of radio dolls, which I always imagined were about to open Bakelite eyes and articulate Mama with perverse innocence. Contrary to the Hippocratic virtues of carnation stalks and the bodiless Swiss croaking a strange Morse code of letters and numbers on the apparatus, as soon as I began to explain the structure of my poem to him and make the intent of the metaphors clearer, the botanist, bored with rhymes, would disappear in the direction of the Calçada do Combro or the Bica elevator that brought the river to the top of the city to the exophthalmic facades that were like the faces of ancient black women settled in the shadows of their huts, floating in limitless oblivion. So I went along, mulling over heroic episodes, stopping to take notes by lighted silk shops, until I came out onto the square with my statue, Mother, with hundreds of pigeons sleeping on the balconies in ceramic positions and dogs who lifted their legs on the pedestal of my glory, and even though the liquor clutched at my legs and made me drag my feet in a thrombosis walk, I managed to reach a set of stairs between two alleys from where, simultaneously, one could see the monument, the trains to Cascais, and the fishing lanterns of trawlers on the river, and precisely at that moment, dear readers, the Rua do Carmo lighted up with a procession of torches and the laughter of apes, halberds struck the pavement, the adenoids of jennets snorted, and King Sebastian appeared on horseback surrounded by minions, archbishops, and favorites, wearing bronze armor and a plumed helmet, and he disappeared in the direction of the pillory by City Hall followed by a fright of police and night watchmen on his way to Alcácer-Quibir.

When the mulatto woman left him and, along with their son, a chest of spangled dresses, and the paper bag of fake silver rings and Bakelite bracelets, moved to the apartment in Olivais Sul that the owner of the discotheque where she worked had set up for her, Pedro Álvares Cabral, after consulting with the Water Company inspector whose breath would carbonize mosquitoes, decided to emigrate to Paris. Diogo Cão, relieved of checking meters since his arrival back in Portugal, dug some muddy documents out of the bolted baggage under his bed, sat down with him on the steps of the boardinghouse beneath the fever of the doves, and, with his nautical finger pointing to the Britanny coast, recommended Ask the boatswain's mate to land you here, take a good look, here, and that's all he has to know, follow in a straight line, it's a cinch, you'll come to a city with a big, tall iron tower and there you are, I must have a few French shillings upstairs, give me five minutes and I'll get them for you.

Pedro Álvares Cabral, confused by the drunken mariner's descriptions as he kept making Paris bigger with every swallow, attributing the stinking canals of Venice where doges raved on the water to it, the visionary statues of Florence, and the almond-cake cupolas of Moscow under which vampirish Rasputins hypnotized countesses, telling him that on Sundays they guillotined kings in vaudeville shows for the amusement of the populace, would visit his son every week at the Olivais apartment, an unfinished building next to a school playground: the elevator would drop him off on the ninth floor, which smelled of turpentine and wax, he would press the three musical notes of the bell, the mulatto woman, in silvery slippers and a dressing gown with ostrich feathers around the neck, would open the cushioned door for him, and I'd catch sight, admiral sir, of the blue-grass miracle of the carpeting, the play of reflection from the shelves of crystal ware over the bar, the piano with solemn varnish like the coffin of a pope, the drapes replaced by medieval rose windows showing a weight-lifting John the Baptist sunk up to his waist in the transparency of the Jordan, and on top of a carved table covered with a smoked-glass plate, between two Malayan ashtrays, the portrait of a distinguished gentleman, fifty or sixty years old, a cocked hat upon his gray hair, whom my wife respectfully called Mr. Sepúlveda, who'd given her the apartment, presented her with half a dozen fox furs with ruby eyes and shad teeth along with a cook in a pleated apron, five maids who could lift their right legs in unison on a cancan stage, and a strict and masculine Scottish governess, the sister of twelve international rugby players, who taught the child how to use his eating utensils the way they do at court, how to part his hair on the side of his kinky head, and how to greet me with a distant nod of his head the way princes in Great Britain do in their foggy palaces, so I didn't dare get close to him, driven back by his icy waves and ethereal figure of a nobleman ordering me with his little finger to put my behind down on the edge of an easy chair with large mahogany arms and observing me without affection from a kind of velvet throne in the funereal pomp of royal audiences. On Thursdays the mulatto woman would send the cook and the maids out, have the freckle-faced nurse take a stroll with his lordship through the stairs and plane trees of the zoo, parroting in the language of a broken-down vacuum cleaner the names of the hyenas and monkeys, or she would tell her to take him to the Estrela to attend the concert of waltzes by the Philharmonic Orchestra of the Volunteer Firemen of Mealhada on a disagreeable metal bench. Then she would take an aromatic bubble bath attended by a Japanese masseur who rubbed her back with lilac algae sponges, deodorize the swallows' nests of her underarms, perfume herself with essences, soft candles and chafing dishes with African powders in the corners, put on black stockings, dress like Elizabeth I for Francis Drake in a combination of sleeves and brocades, unroll a carpet of violins on the record player, make herself up at the prima-donna vanity in her dressing room, recline in Siamese positions on the velvet cushions of the bedroom, and await the embraces of Mr. Sepúlveda, a widowed gentleman who'd buried his wife in Angola and was pouring boleros into the Lixbon nights pierced by the yellow headlights and tin-can thunderclaps of garbage trucks.

The mulatto woman had stopped working and busied herself turning the pages of fashion magazines with the bored thumb of a person pulling the petals off a marigold for amusement. She would receive the pedicurist, the aetheticist, the hairdresser, the instructor in Good Manners & the Integral Calculus, with her usual indifference, which good fortune was making even thicker, blow on the birthday-candle fresh polish of her nails, looking out onto the landscape of Olivais from her balcony while I tried unsuccessfully to carry on a conversation with my son who was got up as a miniature Henry VIII, answering the timidity of my questions with the neutral face of a diplomat or a jailer, and he would finally emit some incomprehensible phrase as he scratched the ears of a trained setter that had revolting human expressions, and as he listened to him recount those visits on the steps of the boardinghouse, facing the pigeons' paper gray, Diogo Cão stuck his bottle into his pocket after applying an indignant pat to the cork, and said Wait here just a second, I'll be right back, his aimless steps could be heard on the floorboards behind me and Mr. Francisco Xavier's rocking and an avalanche rolled down the steps, followed by a silence, then a second tumble and a painful string of high-sea curses and after an hour had passed the navigator appeared, holding on to the base of his spine, all covered with hasty bandages and with a huge bruise on his chin, he spread his maps out on the grass, fished his astrolabe out of a shoe box that had urchins constantly asking him for silkworms, shot the sun that wasn't there, getting lost in impossible latitudes, and stated, patting his coat in search of the wine, multiplying time zones and subtracting miles, Take passage aboard the first packet leaving Lixbon and in a week you'll be in the Moulin Rouge with an actress on each leg, thumbing your nose at this shit.

Since he didn't have the money for the sea voyage, however, and since he really didn't have a red cent, bumming around after the dry-land seagull refugees from five-star hotels with their walk twisted by huge sword hilts led him to drop anchor in the kitchens of parish halls where spread out on large biblical tables were meals of boiled potatoes in exchange for the solemn promise of instant conversions, Swear on the health of your parents that you will suckle the little blessing of the Lord every afternoon, and he, I swear, Promise that you will say four rosaries every day, and he, peering at the bean pot I promise, he made a deal with the owner of a one-chair barber shop on the Avenida Gomes

Freire who was the chum of a cousin of a Gypsy smuggler, and they arranged a meeting for ten at night in the Flor Dos Capuchos, a lunchroom squeezed in between the Patriarchate and a hospital, with a resigned old man sitting in a corner, with its belladonna tea for the sick, trays of codfish cakes with the consistency of stone, and the Gypsy, dressed like George Raft, loaded down with rings, wearing a necktie of gold rosettes and naked girls, got up from the table where he was conspiring with a partner who was younger but already impressive with his silks and diamonds, came over to me with the smell of brilliantine from his mustache and holding out the shady hand of a cutthroat, You're Pêro Vaz de Caminha's friend, aren't you? Federico García Lorca, pleased to meet you.

The swans in the Campo de Santana were wailing their laments in the pond, locusts were breaking the gelatin of eggs in flower beds, hooded canons were circling in pairs under the cardinal's windows, discussing beatifications and homilies, ambulances from São José were coming and going, tumbling like well buckets, bearing along with their sirens severed legs and other horrible misfortunes. Federico García Lorca introduced his colleague in goldsmithery, busy unplugging one ear with a matchstick, My partner, Luis Buñuel, who was best man at the wedding of all the customs guards in the Alentejo. They ordered cinzanos from a simpleminded character dozing amidst a swarm of labels and the Gypsy smacked his lips, furrowed his brow, pulled at the cuffs of his shirt, exhibited a metallic bracelet, and declared firmly Let's get right down to business, it's twelve *contos* five hundred and let's leave it at that.

Pedro Álvares Cabral went back to Olivais to wheedle the money for the trip from the mulatto woman and surprised her, arms and legs akimbo, stretched out on a kind of gynecological platform like a dissected hare, smothered by a battalion of beauty technicians who were furiously working on the defects in her feet, the calluses on her knees, the stiffness of her joints, an impardonable wrinkle at the corner of her mouth, the hair that had to be combed into casual bangs, the shoulders that should glow from golden palettes, the contact lenses that would soften her eyes, the diamond earrings, and my son and I waiting in the parlor, he probing me with that millimetric attention of a stern policeman, I lost in a watercolor that showed a widow contemplating some coins under the shower of light from a street lamp, until the metamorphosizers withdrew from their quartered victim, as if they had reduced her to a stew of dry, marrowless tibias, and Pedro Álvares Cabral watched his wife get up from her table of plastic improvements just like images in churches in the morning, pulverized by the sun that exploded like a fruit onto the windows in the main nave that showed the beheading of martyrs, so he got up, dazzled, ankles entangled in his sword, took a slow step forward, as if he were walking on water toward that apparition of a lay saint all prepared for the weekly visit of Mr. Sepúlveda in the frame on the piano, and I asked timidly, running the tips of my fingers over her inaccessible atmosphere of powder and perfume, Would you happen to have twelve *contos* five hundred you could lend me?

The son, escorted by the Scottish lady companion, who later on would come to marry a bastard son of Sá de Miranda and was the mother of the famous two-headed child who lived for six hours cursing the astonished hospital nurses from its cradle, took leave of him on the landing, offering him a slender and disdainful hand, and in the lobby of the building, chatting with the concierge on her hands and knees, scrubbing the marble steps, I ran into a gray-haired gentleman wearing a nobleman's helmet, carrying a bouquet of orchids wrapped in cellophane, and putting an American cigarette into a jasper holder. And that was how, in the course of the fleeting instant in which I saw him, I came to know the man for whom you were preparing yourself, perfuming yourself, softening yourself, polishing yourself, the old man whose colored picture on your night table, in a bathing suit at the edge of a pool, you slept next to, as it had never interested you or you had never thought to do with mine, the character who made you dress up for him in the excessive getup of a Spanish prostitute, done up with bustles, emeralds, bodices, petticoats, and Pedro Álvares Cabral pictured him pushing the elevator button, watching the numbers of the floors rise one after the other on the way up to hers, hearing the little sound of the key, the Scotswoman getting the child ready for a strategic session at the movies or an opportune concert at the Estrela while Mr. Sepúlveda put his cigarette in the ashtray, checked the placement of objects and the absence of dust with satisfaction, put his helmet on the sofa, and accepted your body of cologne water, musk, and ostrich feathers, your jewels that dug into his chest, the topaz clasp of your belt that tickled his navel, the oregano smell of your sex that pushed up against him like a clump of magnolias on a smooth river, and into a sweet and damp and weightless weariness of sleep.

The next week I found the two Gypsies in short jackets and arabesque ties in a billiard parlor on the Praça da Figueira, hanging around by the showcases with sugar candy and the doors to toilets that smelled of dead sting rays and potash. Federico García Lorca folded the check in half, rubbing the fold with a ring, buried it in the confusion of forged credit cards and pawn tickets in his wallet, sank into a contemplation of the cues with the expression, simultaneously attentive and absentminded, with which farmers measure rain clouds from the threshold and that moment there was a shout from behind the counter Mr. Luis Buñuel wanted on the phone, and the second Gypsy, bald, ugly, with scrutinizing eyes, said Excuse me and walked through a noisy and confused aisle of old ladies, pots of linden tea, and cream puffs, distorted by the play of green and white reflections from the billiard tables where figures in shirtsleeves, celluloid visors on their heads, were executing a ritual dance around the felt of the tables, beyond which there was a jumble of gratings and sacks piling up. The one with the check was sucking throat lozenges, deeply interested in carom shots and at that point Mr. Luis Buñuel came forward with the scent of Chantilly on his mustache, signaled the bootblack, who knelt at his feet with a vassalage of polishes, put his foot onto a wooden box, asked me, flashing sapphires Have you got a cigarette you could let me have? evaporated into smoke and announced in the jumbled Castilian of transistor smugglers, They called me just now from Granada, the day after tomorrow we'll be sleeping there.

The three of us went out to celebrate into the night of sleeping offices and closed shops on the Praça da Figueira, with the bronze king on horseback in the center and junkies shooting up in doorways, I in the middle and one of them on each side, armed with diamonds and switchblades, laughing with dealers in secondhand records and pornographic magazines in the Mouraria, with the women selling vegetables and taking in the breeze, sitting on steps or little canvas stools, with beetle-browed doormen at clandestine gambling dens in the basements of demolished buildings, and we tore apart the darkness, glass after glass, in an amusement parlor baroque with sports pennants. I beat them nine to one before an audience of pathetic drunks, whose meninges were languidly boiling in the amniotic fluid of the wine, I won again six to four with two goals made by the goal tender's hat, we bought a round for the house in order to make their moribund minds crumble a little more, slipped past the driveway of the morgue declaiming poems, *Verde que te quiero verde, Voces de muerte sonaron cerca del Guadalquivir, Antonio Torres Heredia hijo y nieto de Camborios,* and Federico García Lorca's voice had the taste of oranges, knife blades, lunar olives, and braids of wind. We climbed up along the cortege of sad lampposts on the Avenida Almirante Reis, glimpsing the plaques for oculists and textile shops, repeating in a chorus *Verde que te quiero verde* after a momentary stop at the Cervejaria Portugália for a quick drink at the bar, we got lost among the modest buildings of the Arco do Cego that smother the shambling center for tuberculars and the monument to my comrade Ferdinand Magellan, snuffed out by fever in his stateroom paneled in rare woods, leaving his sailors in his last will and testament a painting by Vieira da Silva and the complete works of Pierre Loti, we went in to suck on Venezuelan stogies in a corner house with veterinarians' plaques on the front, scaled up several floors without elevators, blowing the boiling water out of our lungs and kicking the people snoring on the steps, Mr. Luis Buñuel rapped out a code of taps, distractedly mumbling *Verde que te quiero verde,* and inside there we came across an assembly of macabre Gypsies bedecked in sharp colors applied by the most expensive tailors in Lixbon and plotting a sneak across the border into the realme of León for the killers of Inês de Castro, a trio with the faces of wanted criminals that appear in the newspapers every day alongside the ad for the famous shampoo Caspex, which increases falling hair and wipes out eyebrows and toenails, sought by the Secret Police, the National Republican Guard, and Dom Pedro's private army.

Pedro Álvares Cabral, to whom Mr. Luis Buñuel was constantly whispering One of these days, you'll see, I'm going to get away from all this crap and make a film that will leave them all with their mouths open, left the following afternoon in the van of a radio and TV store without saying good-bye to his son or the mulatto woman or the meter reader for the Water Company, Diogo Cão, most certainly taking his ease at the Apostle of the Indies Boarding House opposite the doves, shooting the sun with his astrolabe and navigating through the mustiness of his maps from an imprecise reading of the stars in search of the azimuth closest to the show-window women of Amsterdam. They had dinner by the side of the road in a restaurant in Montemor decorated with bullfighting banderillas, saddles, and capes, the assassins disguised with false mustaches, which complicated their chicken soup and came off with the gravy, spreading thick oakum bristles onto the beef. The hoods dropped down around the back of their necks and the tips of their daggers cut into the worn lining of their jackets. The hounds of the counts who were hunting wild boar in the area and galloping over the pavement to the gourdlike sound of their hooves, sniffed at the doormat with their blindman-cane noses before disappearing on the run after the unforeseen scent of a wild animal. Diogo Cão was probably dozing in the dampness of the night, belly up, on the steps of the boardinghouse, covered with lice and crusted with dirt because of the small amount of water that he used, crumpling his alcoholic's planispheres and his vermin-ridden ship's logs with the weight of his body while the Apostle of the Indies chased after Tagus nymphs, but when Mr. Luis Buñuel, who was driving the truck, got up from the head of the table with a toothpick in his mouth, I followed him, not feeling nostalgic about anything, chatting with the killers of the king's lover under the cedars of Montemor, which added the thickness of their branches and the feathers of their owls to the thickness of the night, and two hours later we reached the scabby walls of Évora, and later on the border, or, rather, a river without any glimmer that separated twin hills with olive groves and rockroses, to walk, scratched all the while by furze, through endless barren fields, with scoop-wheel animals cutting the silence under scrub oaks. It was then that we ran into a large military array of Castilians protecting a tent that was like a lighted market, with hundreds of standards, flags, and field kitchens, surgeons honing scalpels and prestidigitators entertaining the troops, and a sentry informed us that King Philip was meeting with his field marshals in the High Command trailer, planning the invasion of Portugal, because Dom Sebastião, that useless ninny in sandals and with an earring in his ear, always licking the paper for a hashish cigarette, had been knifed in a drug-dealing neighborhood in Morocco for robbing an English fairy named Oscar Wilde of a bag of pot.

Everything had happened to him in life, from discovering India and cleaning up the diarrhea and vomit of my dying brother Paulo da Gama with my own hands to helping seal up with stearin plugs the coffin of the father of some poor devil who was voyaging to the realme in the hold of a ship after the revolution in Lixbon, from playing cards with my heart not in the game until, as now, coming to live in this place in the run-down neighborhood between Madre de Deus and Chelas that parliament unanimously voted to award me along with a medal and a diploma as payment for my services to the nation and where the king Dom Manoel could come to pick me up on Sunday mornings for drives in his car to Guincho.

During the week, while a municipal gardener trimmed the beard on the hedge and did orthopedic work with some sticks on the gladioluses in the flower bed, a maid paid by the government, with the shield of the republic on her smock, dusted the government allotment of furniture placed against the logs of the wall, teetering desks, file cabinets without drawers, warped shelves, portraits of long-forgotten deputies and prime ministers in pompous poses, the bed of an infantry major that smelled of spermaceti and grease, and the only object that I kept from my countless years of navigation, which is this little chrome bear that a nymph of the Orient, a secretary in the Indonesian administration, the daughter of the god Oceanus and a temple vestal, gave me as a going-away present from Goa, almost at the gangplank, on the condition, my love, that you never forget me, I'm twenty-three years old, I have an appendicitis scar, feel it, and I go by the name of Adelaide da Ressurreição Peixoto. A bear I placed in the center of the dining room table and which would observe me with an imbecilic attention while I swallowed the hake with sprouts, the diet prescribed for me by the navy doctor after deciphering the chits from the analyses, No fat or fried food, my dear count, because I don't like what that liver is telling me. A worthless little bear, the kind that's found along with thousands of others, absolutely identical, on the blankets spread out on the ground at country fairs amidst the protests of piglets and the bleating of sheep, but which reminded me of distant sands, palm trees, breasts of foam, lacquered vaporizers, and the laughter of eternally young maidens.

When lunch was over he would take a stroll through the neighborhood, greeting the ladies in bathrobes who hung out of the dizzyingly high windows on the second floor, he felt the afternoon heat that scorched the sparrows in midflight or he caught the glimmer of the river over the archway of the Ateneu, and at four o'clock he would drop into an easy chair belonging to the State with a chessboard on his knees and play against imaginary opponents in solitary card games whose vicissitudes he jotted down in a dispensary appointment book. He dined on barrel water and caravel hardtack and with all the windows closed and all the ladies withdrawn, he would go back up, dragging the heels of his slippers on the floor, take off, as well as his joints would let him, his belt, his dagger, his doublet, his ferryman's life jacket, and the other appurtenances of an ageless seadog, pluck river lice from the curls of his pubis and ebb-tide nits from the folds in his buttocks, slipping limb by limb into a pair of children's pajamas with little tassles, and when he turned out the light with the switch on the lamp, the sheets would begin to dance like part of a hull in a contradictory Indian Ocean, his shoulder blades became covered with pellagra blotches and Madagascar vibrated, inaccessible, thousands of miles from me, with its huts on stilts and its octopuses with swollen eyelids.

On Sunday mornings, if the sun was shining, the king Dom Manoel would blow his horn out on the street inside an ancient rusty Ford with a convertible top, and the neighbor women, half-awake in their nightgowns, would peep out at the monarch with his tinfoil crown on his head and wearing an overblouse with the sleeves rolled up, waving at Vasco da Gama with his scepter, ordering him to come down so they could be on their way along the Marginal to talk about the Orient with a crippled bouncing of springs, enveloped in spirals of dark smoke from the engine.

Beyond the Boca do Inferno, on whose rocks fishing boats that had lost their way were being impaled along with a rain of tuna fish and sardines, they put into a peaceful esplanade for an octogenarian snack that age had reduced to crepes, pancakes, and mashed potatoes, and, squatting on a crag, hated by the sea birds of the slopes, they went on about voyages, the intimate merits of Chinese women, and the affairs of the kingdom. Dom Manoel, the crown on his knees, scratching the hollow of his skull with a fingernail, was bemoaning the misery of this life, hell, look how we're getting old without realizing it, look how we're no good for anything, I'm not exaggerating, damn it, for anything, you try to climb up a mast and you can't, you try to read a telephone book and fat chance, look how age makes the sound of the waves

breaking on the shale down there turn sad, the anxiety of a hospital at night, look how our noses have got thick, huh, our fore-
heads yellow and wrinkled, our cheeks covered with cabbage-slug
saliva, maybe it would do us some good to go to the circus tonight, the circus helps, if you stand at the foot of the palace you
can always see contortionists and trained critters, I'm crazy about
contortionists, don't you like it when they bend their elbows
backward, and then it smells so strongly of ammonia that we
can piss in our pants without any shame, what do you say we
reserve a box for later on?

They bought seafood tarts in Carcavelos, the king dropped
him off at home because the xylophones and shouts of the clowns
brought on suicide attempts in Vasco da Gama, and he went
on down the street in his damp-straw smokescreen waving good-
bye with his scepter. The count stumbled up the steps, exchang-
ing his uniform for the pajamas of his solitary card games. While
ants took over the dinner prawns on the kitchen table, he decided what cards were wild, shuffled the deck, dealt them out
to the imaginary players, squinting at the cards with the rapa-
cious eyes of Mississippi riverboat gamblers, and while the game
went on and he counted his winnings, he was thinking about
his drive to Guincho with the king, about the people selling
wicks, lupine, and calfskins along the side of the road, the tin
roofs, transistors, and the stands at improvised summer markets,
the traffic policeman who ordered them to stop by the motel in
Oeiras, got off his motorcycle, slowly taking off his gloves, the
six hundred exhausts on his Japanese bike, and he raised his hand
in the vague gesture of a salute, Your papers.

The sea could be glimpsed through a glimmer of fins along
the edge of the bushes. Whole families were returning to Lixbon

in long weary lines and Dom Manoel was looking for his wallet in his blouse, in the pockets of his ermine cape, inside the suit of armor that he was carrying on the rear seat of the car along with arrows for a crossbow and an Israeli machine gun, and he ended up showing a parchment with Gothic characters that was wrapped in successive layers of dirt on the dashboard that the policeman examined disinterestedly as if looking at the ad for a hearing aid thrust at us as we come out of the movies by ragamuffins favorable to noise.

"It's written there that I own this country," the monarch informed him simply, pointing to the letters.

An old man in a sweat suit who looked like Miró was jogging, on the verge of collapse, along the sidewalk, followed by an asthmatic terrier. On the side facing the waves the buildings of the Marginal were huddling against one another, frightened by the poisonous perfume of the water, fleeing in the direction of the park and the gasoline pumps of Santo Amaro ahead of the crescent of fog coming from the beach. The policeman suspiciously took in the tinfoil crown with plastic emeralds, Dom Manoel's straggly hair and street-carnival getup, before returning the parchment and unhooking a kind of catheter tube with a balloon on the end from his hussar's jacket.

"Do you think this is a holiday or something? In any case, just give me a little blow into this to test you out for alcohol."

While His Majesty, a vein bulging on his neck, was puffing up the liquor apparatus, Vasco da Gama, even without the help of the eyeglasses stuck away in the pocket of his vest, took note of the arrangement of masts on a ship anchored in the Tagus, with flags furled, waiting for a wind in order to go down to the river mouth on its way to archipelagoes inhabited by strange volcanoes and inconceivable vegetation. The statue of Christ the King, alongside the bridge, was opening the reinforced concrete compassion of its arms for seagulls and airplanes. The policeman studied the balloon, wrote down grave phrases on a printed form, and slowly walked around the automobile, pointing out violations, before resting his elbow, heavy with threats, on the edge of the door.

"Failure to present the documents required by law," he enumerated with saccharine cruelty, "not to mention the lack of rearview mirrors, mudguards, windshield wipers, spare tire, or exhaust pipe. There's also the misalignment of the headlights, no bulbs in the parking lights, and the oil our friend here is dripping onto the pavement so people coming behind him will butt their heads into a tree. On top of it all, the alcohol test shows positive for light wine. Pull that piece of tin off the road so the wrecker can haul it off to the junkyard tomorrow, and if you gentlemen will get out of that rattletrap, I've got a nice little room waiting for you at the stationhouse."

"I just told you a while back that I'm the owner of all this," Dom Manoel argued in a thread of a voice, placing the crown on his head.

A blackbird hopped out of a boxwood, crossed the road, and disappeared mockingly down the motel driveway. It seemed to me that the Tagus had the smell of the odor of your body when you wake up, indifferent to my love for you. The Civil Government cells were lined up in the basement of an ancient building with shutters in and out of whose courtyard a procession of paddy wagons and court clerks came and went. They locked us up, along with a pot for urgent micturition and a draft

that made the hair on our necks stand up as a premonitory warn-
ing of the flu, in the compartment next to the one where they'd
chained up the Jew António José da Silva, the author of skits
about stuffed shirts, who had fun playing naval battles with Vasco
da Gama, cheating with double-barreled ships so as to win more
quickly while he awaited the gloomy visit of the friars from the
Inquisition, their heads covered by pointed hoods and with large
crucifixes on their chests, who would visit him at odd hours,
scuffing their sandals, in order to prepare his soul for the bonfires in the Rossio.

For forty-eight hours the count and the king endured a
lighted bulb in the ceiling that prevented them from sleeping,
deafened by the sirens on the patrol wagons and the chanting
of the friars, who would intrude into the heretic's cubicle with
the macabre persistence of scarabs in a corpse. And it was when
they were already confusing night and day and the date began
to entangle them in perplexed conjectures, when the shadow of
a nostalgia for ships glided, sailing adrift, along the whitewashed
wall that they were taken, unshaven, without having bathed or
brushed their teeth, without having perfumed themselves with
the essences of their status as noblemen, without taking leave of
the double-barreled jokester busy with a new farce for puppets,
to a room in leprous stucco called Police Court, furnished with
several narrow sacristy benches on which an audience of on-
lookers and idlers was seated, your people, the poor of Lixbon,
Milord, who in the year fourteen ninety-eight had crowded
onto the beach at Restelo to see me leave, those grave faces
etched by the disillusionment of misfortune, those hopeless eyes,
that tattered clothing, the people who expected nothing from
You or me after not having expected anything from anybody,

even by some miracle, and they stared at me with expressionless faces with which their children observe them before nailing up their coffins, your race of heroes and seafarers, Majesty, who wasted away from coconut-milk diarrhea in Guinea, wandered, drinking stagnant water, over the dunes of shipwreck in Mozambique and swarmed in the taverns of Madragoa and Castelo, discussing takeovers of schooners and comparing the haughty diameter of the breasts of Your Highness's lovers, using the mugs of red wine as a standard and the concubine who lives in Mouraria and always goes about barefoot with the broad furrowed feet of a gadabout, the wife of that marquis he sent centuries ago to Macau to oversee the installation of his own cuckoldry, the black slave girl with the cheeks of her rear end run through by a thin silver ring, the French slut who danced in the second row of chorus girls in a cabaret in Marseilles and whom State money set up in a home in Lapa bigger than an embassy, with willow, swimming pool, sauna, gymnasium, and seven hundred thirty-five different deodorants, not to mention the Austrian princesses, the Galician chambermaids, and the worker from the spinning mill in Guimarães, the only one perhaps that you really loved without ever demanding anything no matter what and who ended up immigrating to Germany, married to a doglike shoemaker.

At the Police Court, in addition to the aforementioned audience held back by the main rail of a poop deck, there was a speaker's pulpit for a greasy judge, shaking feathers off his robe, lesser places for the prisoners, lawyers, guards, and some kind of attendants dressed in black surplices as for a spiritualist mass, who were typing with one finger, carrying cases back and forth, and calling witnesses who were herded together like goats in a

nearby pen that smelled of hay and uncarded wool. Before we
went in, Dom Manoel polished his crown with his handkerchief
and tightened the ribbon on the ermine cape that said ATELIER
ASSUNÇÃO on the lining around his neck, and both of us, with
daggers and polka dot socks, he weakened by the cares of power
and I devastated down to the architecture of my bones by the
monsoons of the Orient, were called, following the case of a fight
between two women selling chickens on the street and before
the sentencing for passing bad checks of the traitor Miguel de
Vasconcelos, who would be stabbed to death on the first of
December by a group of disgruntled petty noblemen, facing the
judge with the feathers who began by ordering the monarch to
take off the fake emeralds out of respect for the court and to
hand the yellow-painted pipe that was his scepter over to the
bailiff and then for the first time I saw the oakum curls of Your
Majesty's artificial locks and I suddenly understood the extreme
emptiness of command, no matter how many monuments are
built at the anchorages of caravels conquering the world.

A gentleman in glasses, with a speech defect, stood up and
proceeded with a florid accusation in which he labeled us sinister criminals, irresponsible violators of the traffic code, of democracy and human rights, after which he sat down again,
piercing us with his fluted triangular eyes, which the monarch
answered, not saying a single word, with his look imposing the
end of the universe, the same one with which he listened to the
provincial speech of the traffic policeman who was now detain-
ing the afflicted faces of apprentice seamen picked up at random on the streets of Lixbon at night and taken to Sagres to
learn the turbulent mysteries of the trade winds of the sea, the
same royal arrogance with which he tolerated the judge, furi-

ously scratching boils on his neck like a chicken, asking us from up on his worm-eaten tower of a sacred orator, Do the prisoners have anything to say? the same serenity with which he cast his eyes over the anonymous audience of his subjects, and he adjusted the cape on his shoulders before answering, with an absolutely innocent calm, without even forcing his voice, which, however, could be heard without any effort, with a king's unanswerable clarity, in the most secret crannies and dustiest cubbyholes of the courtroom, making stenographers and clerks tremble at the writing desks of their daily arid eight-hour melancholy of warnings, intimations, and evictions:

"I can only repeat that all this crap belongs to me."

The judge forgot about his afflicted neck in order to examine him better, leaning forward, his mouth open and cupping his hand like a deaf person, the attendants froze with shock, the audience of idlers fluttered from wall to wall, the chicken vendors who were continuing their interminable argument and under whose aprons combs and wings peeped out, turned their masks of fearsome buffaloes toward us, and the Pilate, dumbfounded by that absurd affirmation, leaned back in his chair of scarlet velvet, scratching the boils on his temples, and remanded us, dictating our frightening sentence to a myopic typist, to the outpatient clinic of a hospital for the hallucinated, with an aim to ascertaining the cerebral labyrinths of a moribund monarch and a dying navigator smelling of the nutmeg of old men and with cone-shaped goatees like the woeful rabbis of Estonia.

So the very next day, escorted by a court official, we suffered from eight in the morning to three in the afternoon, along with fifty more Copernicuses, in a kind of cellar with a window at the end, where a nurse clutching a hospital card in her hand would appear from time to time, calling one of the scientists who, with a sports section under his arm, snorting astronomical equations of the tenth degree, would disappear into the cabinlike office where the clear octopus outline of a doctor was soaking.

The number of Copernicuses was slowly diminishing, each one of them furnished with a prescription for pills against motion sickness of the earth, and when they got rid of the last and most firmly convinced of them all who tried to imitate movement of the planets of the solar system with the tips of his fingers, a sound-chamber voice called out our names and the judge's man, crushing his cheap cigarette on the sole of his shoe, shepherded us into the shadow of the doctor's confessional, not the royal physick doctor, versed in tidal impulses and lupine broth for the pains of childbirth, pulling on the tongues of princes and recommending diets of cockle juice for the tonsils to ladies of the court, not that usual barber in an anachronistic frock coat who pulled molars with a pair of pliers during palace soirées, taking advantage of pauses by the troubadours, but a lady of understanding and with the benign look of a person collecting for cancer, who ordered that the monarch be given back his crown and ridiculous scepter with the apology of There you are, Highness, please, and she restored the lands, the cattle, and the castles of our status and spoke to us respectfully, with her bows, her complete agreement with us, her Why of course, her Perfectly, her Good heavens where has such a thing ever been seen? her Certainly, my dear count, a person goes through horrible difficulties discovering the sea route to India and bang! a doctor who bowed with infinite respect on taking leave of us, Until we meet again, noble sirs, she patted us on the back, guaranteed, very serious, to bypass the court, This stupid accident will be resolved immediately, I'm going to call the ministry right now, a doctor who stood watching with compassion from her office for curing stellar manias, a doctor who continued watching us in the same way when eight orangutans in smocks pounced on us, forced us to the floor, did us up in straitjackets, drove us out with kicks, just imagine, word of honor, kicks, to a stone cube with successive iron-plated doors where over the entrance it said SECURITY PAVILION and which looked like a bullring without bulls, where they had dozens of locks and bolts to prevent us from escaping, made us change our noblemen's clothes for asylum pajamas and canvas slippers, locked up in a metal closet the crown, the ermine, the cheetah doublets from the Parque Mayer, my tanker captain's instruments, shaved our heads, mustaches, and beards and finally left us in an inner courtyard with very high walls where the fifty Copernicuses with prescriptions were idly wandering about in pajamas just like ours, shading their eyes and consulting the length of the shadows and the position of the sun.

There are always those wretches prepared to pay to sleep with a woman, even if she's as old as I am, idiots who escort me to my room, climbing up five floors without an elevator, clutching their hands to the bouncing of their dying hearts, who fold their trousers along the crease, arrange their shoes side by side under the chair, sit down on the bed after giving me the money, requesting My dear lady just let me lay my head on your lap, fondle me the way my aunt used to when I was little, things like that, while they eagerly touch me on the dry membranes of my pubis and on the few graying grasses I have left there, and by no means are they young customers, ceremonious lads crumpling the five hundred escudos of their allowance, but well-dressed engineers and businessmen, with children, jeweled stickpins, and polished shoes, or divorced high school teachers attacked by the insidious anguish of solitude, the abandonment of people who dine alone at the kitchen table with a weekly magazine propped up against a bottle of red wine. For a month after Diogo Cão left I would take care of five or six of that kind every night, I was maternal and tender the way they wanted because I'd close my eyes and imagine the admiral, equally nude and defenseless, lying on the sheets of my endearments where the others, hugging me, came off, weeping for the joy they didn't have at the same time that I dried their faces with a corner of the pillowcase, swore to them that this life, my dear, is a long way from being a foster mother, what a silly notion, tomorrow, when you wake up, you'll see, you'll feel like a different person, I'd help them pull on their drawers and button up their shirts, look for their shoes in the dark, brush the dandruff off their shoulders, and when the last one has left, his Adam's apple leaping up and down like the Ping-Pong ball in a diver's tube, I'd pull up the covers for sleep, hide the profits from my work as a consoler in a hole in the wall concealed behind a print of Saint Philomena, wrap the hot-water bottle in its cotton cover, and lie there thinking about the poor unfortunates of the next day who would wail from the depths of the pillow about the weariness of it all, madame, just tell me what I can do about it, while Loanda was waking up among its palm trees, crisscrossed by white birds from the bay.

An airline employee who gave vent to such miserable afflictions of a betrayed husband on Wednesdays that the old woman, out of pity, took him with her not to the boardinghouse room but to her thatched-roof hut in Ilha in the district with the wooden shacks of prostitutes from the homeland who with the revolution had disappeared into the jungle or the city or onto the sailing ships returning to the realme, in the midst of convulsed tears and muffled snorts, despairing over the flight of his wife to Rhodesia in the company of a Mexican gravedigger, had arranged a tourist-class seat to Lixbon for her, by a window so she could go into ecstasies over the ocean and its ships from thirty thousand feet, a smooth and colorless surface instead of the thick soup of concrete waters of Africa that rolled its soft back of a tame animal over the roots of coconut palms, and I, ticket in my purse, let him go on inside there in his socks about the twisted wiles of female defenses, Just look, madam, how ungrateful and thankless the bitches are, why just last month I put the car in her name and she screwed me, hit me over the head the first chance she got. I took a walk through the abandoned shacks invaded by scorpions, beetles, and wild vines, I saw a bark going off in the distance, I saw the monkeys with human eyes from Cabinda hanging from the mango trees, I saw the cabarets and seafood restaurants where crabs were devouring the empty showcases, I convinced the UNITA militiamen to let me pass after a private conversation behind a wall with the corporal in charge of the patrol and who, in order to understand my arguments better, probed the openings of my panties, and the next day I came ashore in Portugal, all for the love of an old man with a passion for Tagus nymphs and who, armed with a stick against jellyfish and other aquatic excrescences, would search at dawn for nymphs in the flotsam on the beach.

At the Water Company they couldn't remember any inspector by the name of Diogo Cão because the demands of socialism, you know, ma'am, don't allow us the time needed for bureaucratic updating. Ship chandlers didn't know him, except for the owner of a cod boat from Newfoundland who wrinkled his brow in useless concentration, Diogo Cão, Diogo Cão, I swear that name rings a bell, did you say Diogo Cão? It wasn't on the list of navy admirals, as a clerk at the Registry informed me as he ran his pencil down the alphabetical roster, and I only saw his oval portrait in high school history books, decorated with eyeglasses and horns drawn in ink by cruel students, so I decided, having no faith in bureaus of the State, to look for him all by myself in bars frequented by stevedores and dock workers, in dives with tiles that were filthy with the brown maltha from ships, with one eye on the horizon and the other on the checkerboard and strips of sand along the edge of the city where fat nymphs, like goddesses out of Rubens, are stuck in the mud in the inert poses of drowned cats.

I sought for weeks on end from the Alfama to Pedrouços, always near the water and the hulls of the anchored caravels, just like the ones on the ceramic plates in the Malveira market and hung in living rooms on wire hooks among rag dolls and the photographs of a fireman. I asked about him among the fishermen along the shore with their toes connected by membranes of tar and among the lily-colored transvestites by the mulberry trees on the Avenida Vinte e Quatro de Julho, and they all repeated to me, confused, in schoolboy voices, Diogo Cão, Diogo Cão, wasn't he the graybeard who discovered Madeira? and I would explain to them patiently no, child, he didn't discover any Madeira, he was just a captain on the African run, the one who went up the Zaire delta with the king's ships, and who barely got back to me, wheezing with swamp fever, pale from nausea and vomiting, smothered in blankets with every coat in the house on top of him and a fever of at least a hundred and four until he blinked a little with the fifth or sixth quinine pill, a poor admiral with a wine flask in his pocket and musty maps of the Congo coast in his trunk, a squire of the sea who checked water meters in Loanda and exhaled the irretrievable shipwreck smell of bilge rats. I found a street with his name and the probable dates of his birth and death, a bust in the sculpture gallery of the Geographic Society, invented by a cretin of a sculptor who imagined that the navigators were a strange breed of effeminate Herculeses in bangs, homosexuals from Caparica instead of the old men worn down by treacherous tempests and undiscovered diseases that they were, I got myself a room in the Terreiro do

Paço neighborhood with the idea of keeping a better watch on the ferryboat machinist's mates and I brought occasional sailors and clerks from the Identification Bureau to the estuary of my bed from where the geometric arcades of the square and the wings of the gulls could be seen, and between kisses I involved them in subtle questioning about the whereabouts of the heroes.

I never came upon such bitter men, however, as in that painful period when packets were returning to the realme loaded with disillusioned and wrathful people whose only baggage was a small bundle in their hands and an incurable sourness in their breasts, humiliated by their former slaves and by the plumed pomp of cannibals. The colonists who didn't manage to leave for Brazil or France were like angels who'd lost the skill of flight and were shuffling their earthbound feet through the saddest districts in the city, made up of slopes that led nowhere, baroque pillories, and disoriented stairways where even the balconies on the buildings with their red flowerpots and clotheslines were like backyards in the outskirts. An occasional tropical seraph in a helmet, a tulle veil over the back of his neck, and a wide-mouthed musket for killing crocodiles, would sometimes divest himself in front of me of the uncomfortable cartridge belts that crossed his chest with rows of bullets, take off his leather puttees for protection against jungle vipers, and drop on top of me on the bedspread like the castaways that toilet attendants release from their canvas wrappings onto autopsy slabs. I would revive them with my careful and unhurried wisdom out of their many years as men until I saw a swelling on their backs and watched the wings of their status stretch from wall to wall, I would caress them with the astuteness of maiden aunts and arid-looking cooks in the vessel of whose hearts the living broth of blood still bubbled,

and as soon as their eyes grew smaller, consumed by the innocence of infancy, and their lips burst into orphaned sobs, I would
squeeze their kidneys with all the strength of my hands and ask
in a low voice, in the lingering secret of declarations of love, Do
you know by any chance, my sugarplum, anything about a certain Diogo Cão, a fellow given to drink who'd come from Angola
as an inspector for the Water Company and was hanging out
from one bar to another, astrolabe in hand, searching for the
azimuth of booze?

The woman sought him with the stony stubbornness of
old people, deaf to arguments and reasons, guided by her smell
of passion. She bought third-of-a-page ads in the newspapers,
dug through the files of the civil registry in hopes of the non-
existence of a death certificate that would have hopelessly ruined the only reason for going on of one who'd spent countless
years in the misery of boardinghouses, she went to a detective
agency where an efficient gentleman, hat over his forehead, was
polishing his nails in a revolving chair. The investigator demanded an advance for microfilming and out-of-town trips,
jotted down some hieroglyphics in the margin of a magazine,
and slurred some orders barked into the telephone without even
making the cigarette holder between his teeth quiver. Sitting in
the corner of a compartment velveted with dust in a chair that
moaned birth pangs under her buttocks, the client pushed away
a little clothes moth seduced by the low-cut neck of her white
dress, and she was amazed at how the efficient gentleman could
live in that indescribable disorder of a building in ruins without
asthma. When she came back the following week with an ever-
lower cut and more fiery neckline, with an aim to find out what
progress had been made in the search, she came upon a coffin

shop in the office with broken blinds that had belonged to the Sherlock and the clothes moth, reeking with the funereal outpourings of gladiolus sprays and the odor of the little wax hands of sick people's pledges. A serious little girl with a starched collar on her mourning dress was taking care of the establishment beside an altar with electric torches that stood watch over a nonexistent decedent. No one remembered the investigator or the insect, and a clockmaker seven doors down, with a lens fastened to his forehead like a friendly unicorn, assured her, shouting through the ungoverned peeps of the cuckoos popping out of their carved windows, that the mortuary establishment had been prospering there ever since the neighborhood had been settled, and that the business about an investigative agency was nothing more than a fascist calumny designed to discredit the block. The woman, lost in the midst of hands that proclaimed the day or the night, according to the aberrant originality of their maddened mechanisms, thought for a moment that she'd been deprived of the compass of her reason, laid out on the sands of dementia.

"It's possible that I'll run into him in the old folks' home where they'll take me someday," she consoled herself amidst clock faces with Roman numerals that looked like the ring of lashes around a cyclops's eye.

That same night, confident of the inevitability of a hospice, she bestowed her joys for free on a class of agronomy students and a former cabinet minister who'd been courting her for a long time unsuccessfully, overcome by a passion for her circus ugliness. As far as can be recalled, she never took such care in the perfection of her work between the sheets, losing herself in a delicate weave of provocative and outlandish details that led the students to impossible delights that they would remember for the rest of their days and the politician to the brink of a fatal collapse, prevented at just the right moment by the smooth waters of a tender anchorage. But she awoke all alone, as always, in the gilded metal bed overlooking the canoes on the Tagus and into a sunless day, inside of which traffic seemed to be moving and floating in the cushioned mystery of shadows. The transparency could be noted through the walls along with the inside of houses and in that way she discovered what she already knew, that is, the jealously guarded deceptive domestic secrets the way the skeletons of sparrows can be perceived under the lining of their feathers, and the perspective of the streets, dissected by the light, was a procession of multiple diverse intimacies devastated by the amber of a pitiless clarity. Only a Saudi tanker anchored in the river remained stubbornly opaque, closed in over its mysterious Moors, flown over by albatross cartilages and resting on fugitive fishbones. During early morning hours like that, as usual, moreover, in Lixbon's autumnal anemia, the woman felt herself attacked by unwavering convictions and confused premonitions that made her head simmer in girlish exaltation and helped her to discover in the room small objects that had been lost a long time ago and hidden in little crannies in the well of her memory. Her body would effortlessly take on once more the easy precision and the smooth agility of adolescence, her eyes, rid of the cataracts of age, broke down the fibers of the light one by one, like crystal prisms, the whole universe was suddenly located once more within the reach of her hand, so in one movement she took off the garters and professional finery that men would fondle in an urgent drive of desire, and by the window put on one of her fearsome low-cut gowns, spotting from that attic lookout the armada of fishing trawlers from Alcácer-Quibir gathered together by the Column Docks under the command of a blond boy who was to save us from the Spanish occupation. She adorned herself with the usual necklaces and earrings of a pathetically dull silver while down below there was gathering, followed by *crow bones,* an absurd army of Alentejans in sheepskins armed with rakes and razors, Algarveans advancing to the rhythm of festive accordions, colorful Minhotans, Transmontans chiseled out of Douro basalt, and Lixbonian hoodlums with padded shoulders and cotton muscles. She powdered the wrinkles of her face, listening to the melodies of the bands, the E flats of the ukulele orchestras, and the tubas of the palace pages, with royal pennants and banners decorating the instruments. She lengthened the tips of her lashes with a tiny touch of pencil when Dom Sebastião, surrounded by a throng of nobles and businessmen in frock coats, took his place on the ferryboat *Palmelense,* with wooden buoys all around its hull. With the light step of a street urchin the woman descended the stairs of a conservatory converted into a whore hotel by a Neapolitan fairy who always carried with him a hand-cranked phonograph, the 78 rpm records of the late Enrico Caruso, and a portrait of his mother in a porcelain flowered frame. She elbowed her way through the crowd of unemployed who were watching, unrolling streamers, the departure of the squadron, deafened by the diesel engines, by the sextets playing Viennese waltzes, and by the owl-like laments of the loading cranes, and she went wandering aimlessly through the colorless city sunken in the glass jar of sunless days in which things happen one after the other in the aquatic muteness of coral reefs. She reached the Avenida da Liberdade like an eel,

without lingering at the theater posters that guaranteed two
hours of unreality at reasonable prices and did it about five times
more than my long caresses and my awful octopus varicose-
veined legs. At two in the afternoon a touch of sun finally lit up
the grass in the park by the divorce court, and the walls of windows immediately got thicker and people's thoughts became
dressed in the shell of a cheap movie that obstructed the visual
comprehension of the mechanism of ideas. Even so, pushed by
an arm that wasn't there, the woman went stumbling aimlessly
along the sidewalks of Lixbon and in the crystals of her own
recovered uric acid, which made walking difficult and stiffened
her backbone, transformed into the umbrella of a provincial
priest with ribs as painful as grouper bones. She walked along,
indifferent to the streets, thinking about the agronomy students
of the night before, their clay faces annealed by fear and the absolute panic of their haste. She entered and left a church with
dramatic rose windows, distracted by the ghost-train shapes of
saintly images hanging blessed in glass and destined for the cast-
iron nightmare of candelabras. She wandered through the garden of the Panamanian consulate amidst exiled dictators and
parrots who intoned denaturalized refrains in coconut palms.
She was seen in the hopeless wards of São José Hospital, contemplating, without noticing them, the measureless noses of the
patients, and she ended up, with an aim to resting her corns put
to sleep by the stiffness of her shoes and calming down her pal-
pitations with a cup of warm tea and a piece of cream cake, in a
tiny pastry shop on the Largo da Estefânia, sunk in the darkness of a ship's hold, where she could barely make out the outlines of the tables at first or the small window to the kitchen
beside which a glede nearly as big as a man took off from the

wire of its perch. She flopped down onto a Formica chair whose cracked back abutted other cracked chair backs and was putting sugar into her tea when the sleeve of a coat brushed against her chin as she reached for the box of paper napkins, and immediately thereupon to her right she heard the roar of a tremendous clearing of the throat enveloped in a halo of cheap liquor. The sun had transformed the doves into doves and the trees into trees once more, hiding the ramifications of nerves and arteries that withdrew bashfully into the absurd knowledge of encyclopedias. In a city once more irreducibly concrete, bereft of the wide-open shame of families, the woman rusted away by arthrosis and ruined vertebrae turned her low-cut neckline around to insult the throat clearer and came upon the tongue quivering from decades of wine, the dirty fingernails, and the legendary beard of Diogo Cão, his hair uncombed by the squalls of shipwreck, and the outline of the flask of alcohol meant to scar over the incurable wounds, of which no one ever spoke, left by the disillusionment of the frustrated loves of sirens.

The Water Company inspector didn't recognize her: all there was room for in his memory, narrowed by strawberry brandy, were some faded recollections of voyages and catastrophic afternoons in Loanda, and he'd become immune to the weakness of sentiment. He was still interested in the Tagus nymphs but in an intermittent and vague way, in intervals from vinous delirium, which he would spend plumbing the cisterns, fountains, and ponds of the city in hopes of catching a glimpse of the troutlike glimmer of nymphs in their chalky bottoms. The rest of the time he would settle down on park benches with his ocean captain's insignia fastened with safety pins to the cuffs of his overcoat, trying to make out unsuccessfully the geometry of the constellations in the sky at three in the afternoon. His body of a landlocked Neptune had deteriorated during those months of dereliction ever since his return from Angola: he had boils and bald spots on his head, he'd lost twenty pounds, he was incapable of determining the tonnage of ships from twenty yards away, he had only two teeth left in his lower gums, and his breathing was shallow, like that of a baby chick, coming in swift, painful gasps. The woman became filled with consternation in her neckline when she became aware of the fact that the mariner with whom she was passionately in love was gradually turning into a stuffed museum saurian. Nevertheless, she paid for his drinks without his seeing her, asked the waiter in a low voice to substitute tap water for alcohol in the seventeenth round, tolerated his drunkard's stubbornness, told them to bring him a roast beef sandwich, which he rejected with a wave of his hand in a gesture of ill-tempered pride, and she left discreetly behind the sailor as the newsies on the street hawked the latest edition and Moorish slaves trotted down to the Baixa and, fascinated by the swarm of Indian dramas, into the twenty-four-hour movie theaters on Restauradores. Making use of her age-old experience in the art of manipulating solitary men, she managed to shepherd him to her little room on the Terreiro do Paço, keeping him out of the bars that proliferated along the way like fungus on cheese and the grocery stores where we used to down mugs of green wine, sprawling on sacks of beans.

She was just getting him into bed as he was almost passing out from an unknown intoxication brought on by a few glasses of tap water, when the band of agronomy students knocked at the door, barely recovered from the stupefaction of orgasm. There were about a dozen bashful schoolboys, with downcast eyes and limbs that never finished the indecisive sweep of their gestures as they stood staring at her on the landing with determined and lyrical admiration. The abrasion of age and her knowledge of male weaknesses prevented her from being upset; she serenely covered the discoverer with a sheet that she had embroidered with small flowers on afternoons when there were no customers, applied pomade of sulfur to the green boils and gardenia lotion and carbolic acid to the alopecia on the back of his neck, went over to the landing, taking the hairpins out of her gray braids, removing her plastic jewelry and three dozen coral bracelets, stroked with the compassionate hand that provided us with dreams of ingenuous offerings and broadened the margins of our sad and living flesh the cheek of the nearest agronomist, a redhead with freckles that were all aglow with the combustion of desire, and asked us to leave, with a friendly tilt of her chin:

"I've got my husband asleep in there."

Then, as soon as the troop of disillusioned adolescents was out of hearing on the stairs, in search of an unmarried prostitute who wouldn't surprise them with the unexpected presence of a bearded mate, she double-locked the door so as to be free of inopportune visitors, placed her extravagant rings one by one on the marble top of the dresser as the bulb in the ceiling drew a sumptuous carnival glint from them, pulled her miraculous low-cut gown over her head, unclipped the little lace roses of her succession of corsets, disappeared into a man's Turkish dressing gown forgotten decades ago in her house in Loanda by a customer whom she had forgotten in turn, lay down on the edge of the mattress alongside the commandant, although as far away from him as possible so as not to disturb his belligerent drunkard's dream, switched off the light, and remained in the darkness, not daring to touch him, perceiving through the curtains the ash-colored splotch of the river with its reflections of anchored galleons and the equestrian statue of the king, Dom José, trotting over the obverse of his own image in tranquil majesty. Every minute or so Diogo Cão, attacked by the tarantulas and snakes of drunkards, would snore louder, punching illusory lizards out of his way, and she would calm him down by lisping songs of lighthouse keepers and the meaningless words of children's lullabies in his ear. The room had become impregnated with a gulf smell of worm-eaten wood and wet sails. The floor danced like a deck on a morning of disaster. Her tongue tasted like strands of seaweed and phosphorescent foam, and the woman, belly-up in her bunk of melancholy pleasures and compassionate caresses, was sinking all alone into the wondrous torpor of anticipated Christmases.

She woke up before five o'clock, aroused by a voice of command that went beyond the room and extended out past the building through streets and squares, demanding the immediate opening of the cabin to her astonished eyes still hazy with the weariness of joy. In front of her, standing, gripping a shoe, side-whiskers in disarray and overcoat buttoned at random, the admiral was staring at her with his customary morning lucidity reinforced by the purge of the glasses of water from the night before, and his eyes pierced my emotions and feelings, turned the corners of memory and took measure of my cubicle of a poor Ilha whore in Loanda with a clothesline between two skeletal palm trees, no Tagus nymph in sight, and a cage of parakeets twittering on the porch.

With two strides of a sailor on an uncertain deck Diogo Cão, his memories of a meter reader and nocturnal beggar reduced to the charity of an old woman in a wretched tin-can neighborhood immediately shoved into oblivion along with the cabarets of Angola and the clumsy legs of dancing girls, assumed once more his nautical powers over the thousand rose petals of the winds and the black buffaloes of reefs, leaned out the window with the hem of his overcoat fluttering about his knees, held on to the steering wheel of the windowsill, and roared into the square down below, with his strands of hair pointing to Seixal, startling the beggars in the arcades and the cripples in bolero jackets who were dozing, enwrapped in the calm of the seagulls:

"Taking water astern, man the boats."

His voice still held the authority of past times when he had ordered maneuvers contrary to all nautical logic, obliging crews to obey him without hesitation, with confidence in the roars that shepherded them along. All by himself he subdued mutinous mercenaries, brought barons under control with a simple raising of his eyebrows, and disobedient boatswain's mates hanged themselves from yardarms, and, it might be added, with the round shells of their nostrils pointed in his direction. The woman, meanwhile, remained motionless in bed, the key to the room hidden in a hole in the mattress: she saw a flock of doves spin off in an ellipse, startled by the discoverer's shout. She saw the statue of the king, Dom José I, quicken its slowed gallop. She saw the roofs of the Costa do Castelo shoving each other from the Alfama down in a devastating panic of wounded rhinoceroses. She caught the sinister hydrosulfuric smell of stormy seas in the room. She witnessed a bolt of lightning that came down from the ceiling to pulverize the ceramic chamber pot. She endured the fall of porcelain ashtrays and tin cans that tumbled off the only shelf she had. She gripped the bedstead firmly so as not to be dragged along up against the wall by a typhoon of sheets. And she maintained a perfect calm that she ended as soon as she rose to the surface of the battling bedcovers and freed herself from a curtain that was strangling her neck, with four stern words that dropped into the eye of the storm like a rock into a well:

"Cut that shit out."

Diogo Cao, astonished, sensed in her tone the music-hall resonances of a very ancient accent, and he saw himself again as a child with his hair in ringlets standing before a lady with her hair in a bun and wearing an apron, who was scolding him, wagging her finger, next to the woodstove in the kitchen. He quickly closed the window, reeling with confusion, and out of the corner of his eye he suspiciously observed the woman who was suddenly offering him, at the age of seventy-one, the diaphanous innocence of the past that he kept carefully embalmed, with the lightness of lace, where fading away were the excitement of spinning a top and the timid fingers wet with squid sweat of his first girlfriends, and he was only standing before a misshapen creature eroded by the pitiless years sunken in a storm of covers on an iron bed who was frowning with his mother's anger and ready to melt, like her, into a catastrophe of tender tears.

Without knowing what to do but knowing that he was doing what he should, he dropped the shoe, which fell to the floor with the sound of an empty biscuit tin, took off a sock with red and blue stripes, exhibiting his admiral's hardened goose step with the dancing gait of a river web-foot, and he came over to

me waiting for the usual recriminations, weakened and repen-
tant now, trying to cover up the bottle of wine in his pocket,
fearful of a fatal reprimand. He smelled of bubblegum and bread
with margarine, like all little ones his age whose absence of wisdom teeth still awaited the monstrous levered jaw of adulthood,
and his unending vigor of a centenary adolescent, his undefined fuzz sown with pimples between nose and mouth, and
his Adam's apple caught in the contraction of a sob pained me.
He still didn't know that he was to command caravels off the
cliffs of Africa, planting markers on the beaches, and he was
secretly planning to grow up as fast as possible in order to become a hotel clerk, a messenger, or an astronaut, the kind that
swim head down over the floating dust on the moon. Prince
Henry the Navigator had been reduced to a virtuous and heroic
fable in history books that showed a prince with a romantic
singer's mustache and a broad-brimmed hat sitting on the edge
of a promontory of cliffs and tossing little paper boats into the
waves out of boredom, and he didn't dream of getting to know
King John II personally, the one whom the public school teacher,
standing before the slate of the blackboard under a brass cross,
guaranteed to be a perverse fellow who knifed cousins with the
hateful brutality of high school delinquents. At the time that
Gil Eanes reached Cape Bojador, he left his job as messenger in
exchange for a desire to be a pool hustler, chalking his cue, cigar
between his teeth, to the amazement of sergeants from the neighboring artillery unit, over the shins of chamomile-tea ladies.
During the last year, while preparing for matriculation in vet-
erinary school, with a passion for migraines in tapeworms, he
received at home an officially franked postcard sent from the
palace summoning him for a medical examination for military

service, and shivering from the cold for a whole morning, naked, along with eight hundred other plebeians in a freezing gymnasium, watching the rain fall on the tin barracks roofs, an assembly of barbers with stethoscopes, medieval helmets, and captain's insignia measured the perimeter of his thorax, Inhale, listened with their stethoscopes, Take a deep breath and hold it, damn it, checked his tonsils, felt his appendicitis scar and lack of hernias, and gave him marching orders for Sagres to start him off in a knowledge of the sea under the command of a bilious quartermaster who smelled of shipwreck mold and coriander soup.

In the course of the months of instruction during which he learned to untie knots and stumble down hatchways the prince in the history books would visit them from time to time with his retinue of admirals, friars, astronomers, and geographers in order to check on the progress of the recruits in the difficult art of escaping fire-breathing monsters and avoiding the whistling of hurricanes. The commandant's orderlies hurriedly set up a silk-tassle throne in the middle of the parade ground destined for the royal highness who, unfolding parchments and pointing to folios, recited for us the Morse code of the stars in the sky, how to apply rubber straps to amputees, exterminate bilge rats with rhododendron powder, the influence of the signs of the zodiac on the sexual behavior of sirens, and the importance of sowing islands on the shadowy oceans with painted Indians gripping bows and curare-tipped arrows who peeped out from behind baobab trees. So that after a year Diogo Cão was already exploring the beaches of Morocco, avoiding schools of octopus and the silvery shadows of sardines, and was heading along the coast of Africa, aided in his calculations by a mad math-

ematician who indicated the course to him from the logarithmic table he was holding.

Little by little the personages of uncertain shape that the
public school teacher, sleeve resting on the eraser, was describing
under the unbreathing fish mouth of the copper crucifix, were
coming closer, alive, identical to the tragic likenesses of the statues on their tombs, and they chatted familiarly with me in the
irony of medieval songs, either in the officers' mess in Lagos, playing dice poker over a glass of whiskey, back from all sorts of scurvy
and countless bitter moments, or at court soirées where they passed
the time pleasantly in the light of resin torches, with great hunting dogs urinating on the Arraiolos rugs, as they listened to the
monarch's tasteless jokes and the troubadors' interminable fados.
On those glum nights peopled with effeminate pages and flickering lights he got to know the chamberlain Egas Moniz and his
sons, with tapes around their necks, Saint Anthony, who was
preaching to tuna fish, the chronicler Fernão Lopes, taking his
notes in spiral pads, the irresistible lashes of João Baptista da Silva
Letão de Almeida Garrett, polygrapher and politician, and Dom
Fuas Roupinho, who, right after the first five minutes of conversation, asked for a loan of two hundred escudos and was accompanied by a Syrian bodyguard with a machine gun under his arm
and a tattoo of Arminda cross-stitched on his right shoulder. On
the second voyage, guided by the madman's arbitrary multiplica-
tions, he managed to take his ship to the mouth of a river in Guinea
where caiman gullets and Pygmy poop floated; he saw his first
siren anointing herself with beach lotion in the eleven o'clock sun
and he docked at Dafundo, darkened by the heat like a burnt olive
tree, to fall into the arms of the prince, whose mustache gave off
a soft sweetness of Aramis.

He sailed for decades on end, rising to the rank of admiral, shut up in his cabin with a pile of novels by Agatha Christie on his night table, while the mathematician continued on, gnawing on the tip of his pencil at a little table alongside, with his undaunted shadowy calculations. He found and lost uninhabited and bony archipelagoes covered only by flat bird calls, escaped from herds of whales who lowed ceaselessly like sad calves and fluorescent sting ray that electrified the water and made hair disobey brushes, he saw whole crews succumb to nameless fevers that turned their skin blue and transformed scrotums into little sacks of pus, he suffered from cholera, dysentery, beriberi, from the hateful bite of bedbugs, from malaria, nostalgia, and varices of the esophagus, he grew old studying unknown planets with an aim to determine with absolute precision the cardinal points of the compass, so that when I met him for the first time in Loanda in the cheapest cabaret in the Baixa he looked to be three times his real age, he didn't have a single tooth left in his mouth but his jaws were lined with plastic incisors that clattered when he spoke like the sound of distant hooves, and his skeletal body, wrapped in the ever-present overcoat, reeked with the wretched aroma common to drowned men and widowers. When he abandoned the house in Ilha in search of the Tagus nymphs, tiny marine flowers bloomed in the cracks in the walls and it wasn't unusual to spot a family of lobsters crossing through the sleepy and motionless morning light, feeling household utensils with their nutcracker claws. Caravel cats dozed in the silence of cupboards. Bureaus cracked the knuckles of their joints on foggy nights. A jellyfish whistled in the bidet. And I was afraid to get out of bed and hover like a coral among copper-colored perches and timid flounders that were vainly trying to get in under the crochet rings.

And yet it would be enough for the woman to sit down on the straw bed and watch the sailor out there, with his pants rolled up and his fingers hooked onto his boots, contemplating the surface of yellow sludge that was wetting his feet. The girls were emerging from the wooden shacks and squatting down, holding up their panties with their knees, to urinate their thick morning piss. Birds from the bay were pecking at the porridge of mud that a trawler engine was stirring. The old woman closed her eyes in the small room on the Terreiro do Paço like someone locking up in a chest her collection of worthless memories of sweaty bars, the pinches of coffee-plantation foremen, filthy washrooms with broken toilets, and the huge gold incisors of the bad breath that chatted so close to mine. She breathed in the chicken broth smell of the sea, contaminated by the diesel oil of Tagus tugboats, ran her index finger over the hem of the sheet, agitated by the din of Lixbon, and heard herself declaring to Diogo Cão, with the modulated sigh of a woman much younger than she was, full of enticing resonances, sugary promises, and the certainty of hidden pleasures, What's keeping you from taking off your clothes?

The admiral stared at the reclining woman shackled by the damask mattress and comforters, looked around her miserable whore's room with ridiculous crooked glass-bead pictures on hooks, observed behind her back the activity of cranes and canoes coming and going on the river, and turned again to the creature lying there, noting the details of the barren wrinkles on her legs, her thinning hair, her faded cheeks, the tips of her breasts that were just like diseased nuts, her ostrich feet deformed by twisted high heels, but he was unable to relate her to the taciturn and gentle toad in Loanda, first because immediately upon embarking for the kingdom he'd forgotten her and second because the years and the rotgut had turned his brain into a kind of sandy surface strewn with cones of guano and inhabited by naiads in scarlet garters who kicked out their fat knees on vaudeville stages. He still hadn't managed not to obey the authority of the voice that arose from the pillow, telling him to get undressed, and he went about arranging his duds on the back of the only chair in sight, from the overcoat given him by the doorman of a bar who'd won the wife of his best friend in a lucky poker game, to the waterproof canvas pants of a sailor subject to the fury of typhoons, until there was nothing left but his timid hands hiding his sleeping sex, gun-worm heads under his skin, and a row of moss petals along his spine.

And that was how I saw him again, naked and ever so thin, so many months later, as when he used to sleep in Africa on the mat for drying manioc spread out in the living room or on the porch and I would spy on him from the doorway, sticky with the sugary moonlight of the coconut palms. His knees were shaking more, his fingers quivered pianolike over the shriveled almonds of his testicles, his mouth was cracked with crusts of dry saliva from his pauper's lunches of the week before, and in spite of the obstinacy of my love he looked like an ageless outcast who could wear a top hat over an asylum bib.

Diogo Cão closed the window on the Tagus, making hazy outlines of the tankers, the frigates, and the cripples with violins, seeking shelter under the arcades of the ministries around the square, and the furniture rose up like trunks stacked in the holds of barks on return voyages from the Indies. The thought came to him for a moment that he too would be suspended, weightless, just like a sad suicide, in the shimmering atmosphere where an iron bed danced like seagulls resting at anchor. Nevertheless, because he still felt the splintered floorboards under his feet and his undeniable terrestrial state with no flippers under his arms or along the small of his back, he grew alarmed to the point of asking in a defenseless wail:

"What do I do now?"

He could have opened the window and recovered the day, giving the room back the sound of the cranes, the albatrosses, and the traffic, he could have begun to read meters in Madragoa, stumbling over baskets of fish and the filth that the ebb tide had rejected on the steps of the sidewalk, he could have reached in his pocket to pull out the flask that worked on his head like photographic developer, revealing the crannies of memory and restful solutions that he wouldn't have encountered without the help of wine, but the dimensions of the bed, which grew from minute to minute to the point of blocking his access to the door, knocked over the chair with a crash of ornate vestments, broke the dresser with marble knobs, filled the space of the window frame and the outlines of the ships, and made him step like a befuddled ostrich, elbows tight against his most intimate parts, until the woman aboard the mattress turned a lazy eye toward him and stole him away from the vapors of his anguish with the whisper of an invitation:

"Come on over here."

Diogo Cão, who considered himself reserved by divine determination for the loves of Thetis and who had never believed that the creatures with vast dunelike breasts of metallic scales and codfish tails from Greenland that his boatswains presented him with for the idle weeks of unloading and repairs were waterfront sluts disguised with cardboard artifices, planned to ignore the woman's request in order not to betray the flock of sirens of his regular passion, with cockles in their hair and strings of clam shells around their waists. The bed was threatening the walls of the room, however, the blankets were puffing out, the old woman's smile was getting larger, the necessities were growing restless in the pot, and a small picture of cupids flew off its hook like the leaf of a plane tree in autumn, immediately crushed by an arabesque of brass roses. These supernatural signs upon which the excess flow of water from the faucet conferred terrible proportions and which the woman's sighs underscored with cavernous asthma, decided him. Just as during periods of calm, when his halted ship obliged him to play a disenchanted game of bridge with his pilots, so did that familiar voice, the natural origins of which he hadn't succeeded in making out, however, pushed him toward the unlimited mattress on which, instead of the usual nymphs and muttering Oh child and dropping painted scales the way chickens in a henhouse lose feathers, lay a shapeless creature who was smiling at him under the exaggeration of her lipstick with the grin of a little girl.

From time to time footsteps would approach along the corridor of tiled panels with masonic symbols, there would be a knock on the door, a pause, another knock, and they would go away with diminishing complaints. A guest was hammering in the room next door as if nailing down the lid on the coffin of an adulterous mate surprised on the knees of the plumber when the husband returned from work. The pigeons were seeking out one another with pecks (a throat was coughing in some undefined cranny) on the rooftop statues. Diogo Cão felt a hand run over his chest, fondle him, pinch the peas of his nipples, pause over the hernia of his navel and the sores from a tropical disease that had never healed completely. The fingers reached the keel of his pubis, lingered there the way the tongue lingers on an aphtha, and they finally found it, small and humble, reduced to a dead little rag at rest on one of his thighs, and which the woman made a vain effort to awaken for hours on end.

The window slowly grew dark, the room disappeared into shadowy waters perfumed by my creams, my lacquers, my polishes, my lotions, but the only odor present for me was the promontory vapor of the admiral, the tornado aroma that made his mustache bend like the tops of pine trees over the dunes, and the dampness of the carious caves of his crumbling gums. Lying up against him, squeezing the cordage of his tendons to my neck, one by one I explored the innumerable niches of his body, coming across more bays and inlets and fishing villages than I had ever found on the countless sailors in my life, including the Venetians who brought me a silence of gondolas and the submerged decomposition of doges' palaces, with canvases of saints and bishops on the marble stone of cellar corridors, as gifts.

No sooner had night begun to dissolve in the room into fragments of weightless cloth that the visceral gases of the seven o'clock ferries frightened off, than the woman, when she no longer hoped for anything in spite of the detailed weave of her art, suddenly touched ground against the navigator's immense and unexpected proud mast, which rose up vertically over his belly with all sails unfurled and the calabash resonance of conch shells. On ranging over the nautical monumentality of that penis embellished with insignias and echoes, fascinated, she grew fearful of feeling herself run through by an energy much greater than that of her uterus, which would inevitably break apart as in an Arab torture on the corncob mattress. She tried to move away, crawling along the sheet, astonished by that limitless potency, but the sailor's grip suddenly immobilized her buttocks with the strength that thirty years before had tamed ships' wheels spinning out of control in storms, and inches from her face she suffered a whiff of beriberi and digested rotgut and found herself finally pierced by a huge yardarm that vibrated inside her with the flutter of dozens of royal caravel standards.

It was a memorable early morning that continued on till lunchtime, indifferent to the occasional knocks on the door, the blindmen's concertinas on the square, the engines of the packet boats, and the doves' interminable chatting on rooftop television antennas. A mute and persevering dawn in spite of outside noises that the curtains' veil transformed into the scattered chords of a delirious harmonium, a tender struggle with burning knife thrusts into my body, a restless living tide that made me grip the railings of the bed until one last impulse lifted me up from the mattress deck, raised up my trunk in a huge gyration, and boiling foam flooded my insides with successive thrusts of a pump, drenching the blanket with the juice of its liquor while the pennants went limp and the whistle of the conchs fell silent and the woman found herself again, pacified, in the company of the skinny and inoffensive old man from the Ilha bars of Loanda, impregnated with wine and attacked by his obsession with Tagus nymphs, staring at her from the pillow, unkempt and with a foolish expression on his doglike teeth.

A regular Friday customer, an expediter from Penha de França, divorced twelve years ago, who would wail in my lap for a modest price about the despair of his loneliness in an apartment in Loures, had rented part of a house for her on the Largo da Misericórdia in exchange for two hours of intimate alleviation of his hopeless melancholy. Diogo Cão, called in for advice, approved of the room hard by a tiny parlor just right for storing his maps of Zaire and keeping battered astrolabes, celebrated the sound of bells from the nearby church, which seemed to announce constantly over chimney tops a fire or the marriage of a princess, and he was exultant over the number of taverns in the Bairro Alto where, furthermore, he would often run into the poet António Duarte Gomes Leal with a white camellia on his greasy frock coat, trading republican alexandrines for the confessionary discretion of his drinks and prepared to help him look for Aphrodites in the creels of river fishermen, the pair of them unsteady on their legs and with cunning little eyes that brought them occasional problems with wrathful illiterates. The cubicle on the Terreiro do Paço went back to its original role as a seraglio of maternal caresses and a drain for consolation measured by the yard, and every afternoon and evening, with the scruples of an exemplary civil servant, the old woman would come down from the Largo da Misericórdia and its echoes of the thirteenth century toward the crippled beggars on the Column Docks, abandoning the admiral, reddened by Drambuie embers, in the first lunchroom along the way. She would pick him up punctually an hour later, already sitting on the sidewalk, stinking of gin, and intoning cabin-boy ballads horribly off-key.

The next week, on the advice of the poet Gomes Leal with whom he would take part in maritime serenades, irresistible for sirens, no doubt, but hated no less by the inhabitants of the district who would empty out their washbasins onto their straw hats, roaring threats to call the police, Diogo Cão invited the woman to accompany him to the Apostle of the Indies Boarding House to retrieve his ship's logs, planispheres, and other State secrets that the palace might call for at any moment and which were falling apart in a corner of his trunk at the mercy of a fat Indian with the look of an Aragonese spy in a room where twenty-seven people slept, mingling their swampy nausea and the mushrooms of their nocturnal vapors.

Hand in hand, mutually supporting each other in the confusion of their old age, hearing the years buzzing like cicadas in their ears and suffering the penury of rusted joints, they walked from the cheap bazaars on the Praça da Figueira along the woebegone Avenida Almirante Reis, admiring tie pins in the shape of a gorilla and orthopedic sandals in pawnshops, carefully examining bottles of brandy in cafés, and startled by the sharks at taxi stands all dressed up like Sudanese consuls, around whom a solicitous swarm of vendors swirled. There were oculists by the dozen where diopters mounted up, beauty parlors that dryer helmets gave the absurd look of domestic spaceships, stores with caged hamsters and little dogs, and photographers with doors on the street who disguised children with the look of martyrs or Breton brides and made young girls pose in profile with paper flowers in their hair and the expression of heartless femmes fatales. At a certain point, by the corner of a building under construction that looked as if it were being torn down, hidden by walls murky with dust and watched over by the diaphanous mortuary shadow of buildings in ruin, Diogo Cão, following the trolley tracks, turned down a side street without any show windows except for those of a Methodist bookstore with its prayer books and pious publications, stopping the woman from becoming frightened, dazzled as he faced an establishment with ducal chandeliers dripping little lilac mirrors and Bakelite pendants. They reached the sloping Santa Bárbara square with its workshops without customers and its day-old cakes, trotted along the edge of a hill, slipped sidewise through a gap in a wall into a vacant lot, startled by military bugles, scraped their shins on chunks of tile and unexpected stones, sped across a brush-covered hillside, and found themselves surrounded by fire escapes and the backs of buildings with rear balconies strung out along lumps in the walls alongside the steps to the Apostle of the Indies Boarding House, where Mr. Francisco Xavier, bursting out of his undershirt, was getting set for the six o'clock breezes by dragging his rocking chair to the lobby entrance under a bower of aroused goldfinches.

The boardinghouse was a run-down cube pockmarked by the weather, with plaster cornucopias and baskets around the ceilings, a rococo roof with beams showing, covered with pieces of cardboard, and a cavelike sound in its deserted corridors. In spite of her long existence as a woman of the streets, accustomed to a thousand abysmal penuries and any number of fearsome misfortunes, never mentioned out of habit, fear, or a strange kind of proud modesty, I could never recall poverty such as I witnessed that afternoon, with characters snoring on top of each other in pigsty garrets, children chewing on cockroaches in the corner of rooms, submissive mulatto woman so thin as to be nonexistent, dozens of evening gowns with erotic spangles, torn and mended with thick thread, hanging from the knobs of balconies. An Oriental lady in slippers and with a mole on her forehead was shepherding that inert flock of homeless whores shivering like coffee trees in the shadows from African fevers and with purulent ulcerations, and while she waited in the former ballroom on the second floor for the navigator to gather his precious marine possessions, she wandered about amidst the panels of seraphim in the pantry, sensing tropical drizzle and ticks and the paths of red ants from Dembos, devouring the licorice of dreams in the darkness.

The early painful times in Angola right after the Lixbon revolution rose up again before her with the cannon fire of its diverse wars, the terrified crowds at the airport and on the docks, the nights in cabarets with no customers where a lonely cancan dancer was wiggling to the rhythm of a dying record, the old woman in the coatroom who lent money at interest to the performers, intent on a complicated knitted circle with her glasses on the tip of her nose. The waterfront was like an antiques store where whole families, watched over by the greed of stevedores, waited for the next frigate in the midst of bathroom items. The dim memory she had of the kingdom was a succession of eucalyptus trees and bandstands where the Sunday sound of fifes played ceaselessly, which would shortly be replaced by hundreds of dressers, dented pots, enameled washbasins, and sacred hearts in bas-relief in a street fair of resigned atomic victims. While she searched the streets of Loanda for Diogo Cão, she looked at the deserted dwellings in the sorrow with which railroad workers, picks on their shoulders, contemplate train wrecks. A mangy breeze blew trash and scraps of paper along the alleys of the city, smothering the dry swimming pools where a solitary light crept along the mosaic. Blacks in Cuban uniforms were fighting with machine guns for the São Paulo fort. And the thickness of the shadows that suffocated the palm trees by the bay hid the neighborhoods that had no electricity and which only the eyes of a gecko could penetrate, burying a surface of crates under the howl of dogs.

When the admiral returned to the lobby of the Apostle of the Indies Boarding House, having trouble pushing a hand cart loaded with sketches of imagined archipelagoes and the detailed description of lunar flora, the woman was watching the departure of the mulattoes for the Arroios discotheques, whose signs spread their creamy orange light along the sidewalk. She saw them go down the deserted slope, afflicted by the torture of their hobble skirts, with the gait of penitents disguised as circus acrobats, worried about the stomach of Mr. Francisco Xavier who was barking encouragement and orders at them from up above, galloping in his rocking chair. The dresses hastily fixed with padding and pins, the makeup casually daubed on their cheeks, and their nails, yellow and chipped like the keys of an upright piano, made her gulp with nostalgia for the ingenious and competent French patronesses who had initiated her, at the turn of the century, in the subtle wiles and difficult mysteries of the profession, severe fifty-year-olds with artificial lashes and absolute intransigence, teaching the devices of the trade while reclining like prima donnas on overstuffed sofas to the sound of mirrored phonographs, and making their pupils pretend love slowly and all perfumed, caressing a tailor's dummy as they moaned. The woman, who was fifteen at the time and had braces on her teeth and a childish walk and was as thin and hairless as a stray cat, had learned to give pleasure with just the touch of a caress and to console depressed sixty-year-olds by listening to them with the impassioned intensity of a confessional as she undressed them, peeling down their pants as one would a tangerine. So she pitied the men obliged to content themselves with the unskilled inertia of the boardinghouse mulatto women who lacked professional enthusiasm and deontological refinement, the men who put their shoes on, sitting on the sheets of the previous unfortunate, with the same sharp sorrow with which they'd started.

Mr. Francisco Xavier, who'd acquired the habit of wearing a saint's halo decorated with small bulbs of various colors around the back of his neck, which gave him the dubious look of an ad for a brand of batteries, tried to prevent the removal of the navigator's documents that centipedes and bookworms had reduced to bran, decimating whole continents, a dozen promontories, and the Andes range, arguing that Diogo Cão owed him not only for eleven months' room and board, but that during the tempests of his drinking bouts he'd broken up half the furniture in the dining room and almost all the windows in the kitchen, not to mention the countless mattresses that had rotted away from his death-anticipating naps and their acidic urine like the piss of a dying horse. The woman, however, an experienced litigant, with an indulgent smile, familiar with the primitive childishness of male exaggeration, and who had learned from her French preceptors an intuition for distinguishing truth from falsehood simply by the tonality of the smell of the vowels, even when written, ordered the admiral, deaf to the arguments and threats of the patron of Setúbal, who was enlarging his complaints to the point of suggesting that Diogo Cão was killing newborn babies and the doves on the roof next door with the strength of his breath and that he'd raped a child ward in the cellar with the help of a chocolate bar, Get along with your papers because I've had it up to here with this argument. She warned Mr. Francisco Xavier that if he persisted in bothering her with his tricks she'd waste no time in turning him in to the morals squad as a pimp and a thief, laying before him a gloomy picture of the dungeons at Headquarters, and when the saint announced, despairing for his cause, that the Vatican had beatified him and that the terrestrial casing of his body would remain uncorrupted till time immemorial, she limited herself to responding that a person who knew so little about love would never gain a place in heaven because he'd wasted his existence in an obscenity of rapes without refinement, robbing any companion of the genuine joy of shared pleasures. The Indian, worried about a visit from the precinct captain or the eventuality of a communication to Rome, ended up helping them pilot the handcart over the reefs of the slope down to the square and even proposed that the old woman instruct the mulattoes in collective classes, with a school projector, in the pathways of the pleasures of the flesh and he was already digging into his pants pockets for an advance payment for the inaugual lesson when the woman froze his hasty motions as she explained to him that the only good rule needed by an authentic female consists in understanding that men need a mother all the more in proportion to the number of mothers they'd had, and that only orphans find themselves prepared for the daily reefs of passion. And while they were going off toward home with their nautical papyruses, the chosen of God stood there motionless on the sidewalk scratching his underarm scabies, absorbed by the weight of that immense revelation, with the ampules of the halo going on and off around his face beside the discotheques of Arroios the way he appears, tortured and kindly, in prints in mother-of-pearl missals along with a prayer that guarantees results in countering family spats.

The weight of Diogo Cão's islands and peninsulas, too much for the age of both of them, obliged them to divest themselves, one by one, of whole encyclopedias of archipelagoes and straits on their way to the square with medieval bells, Misericórdia, in whose shadows the Bairro Alto transvestites kept mingling with processions of penitents in sandals who were flagellating themselves with willow branches. As the power of his muscles weakened, preventing him from carrying his library of continents through the streets of Lixbon, the sailor took the lid off a garbage can and poured into it a bundle of tropical rivers that were buried, along with their fauns, their vegetation, their mineral wealth, their meteorological peculiarities, and the depth and characteristics of their beds, amidst leftover grains of rice and packages of cough drops. The whole planet disappeared that way, country by country and meridian by meridian, in municipal trash bins, and all they had left by the time they reached the neighborhood of the Jardim da Patriarcal was a rusty astrolabe and half a dozen newspaper clippings of Phases of the Moon & Tides that the admiral used to better orient the navigation of his caravels. Near the Bairro, in the distance, in a procession of monks who were intoning gloomy litanies and Te Deums, they caught sight of the poet Gomes Leal in a crushed top hat and with a camellia pinned to his frock coat, urged on by red wine, entering a bar lighted by the phosphorescence of a television set. Carriages of marquesses with coats of arms carved on the doors passed us, their axles squealing, to disappear into the Trindade Theater, their lax rear springs shaking like the tail feathers of a goose. Putting on his pajamas precisely at the stroke of two in the morning, Diogo Cão, in long johns, was floating in a kind of deserted limbo of tributaries and river basins yet to be discovered where some prince standing on the edge of some rocky rise was observing the nothingness with Jockey Club mother-of-pearl binoculars. He pulled the toilet chain to assure himself of the reality of the water but no cataract fell down into the bowl. He glanced at the river through the window and couldn't make out the running lights of sloops and ships, replaced by a great black space crossed by the lamps on the bridge. Looking into the mirror he felt the gums eaten away by scurvy and in the glass he came face to face with a perfect set of ceramic teeth that answered his seaman's sadness with a pleasant smile. He finally dropped them into the glass on the night table, turned out the bedroom light, rejected the woman's concerned caresses, and, gnawing on the pumice stones of his jaws, continued staring at the earth that had been transformed into a desert dry of waves and Tagus nymphs where even the wind of the conch shells had finally disappeared.

In order to lodge the ones whose bodies still retained the smell and the larval murmur of the fields of cotton that wild dogs crossed with their chimerical trot among those returning from Africa, the government emptied out a hospital of tuberculars, who went off to cough their weary hemoptyses in public parks, and into the infirmaries with walls displaying scenes of war and pious deeds, impregnated with the death torpor of disinfectants, they poured the colonials, who, bundles under their arms, drifted about the vicinity of the hospitals in search of the remains of some dinner soup.

The man named Luís, who fed himself on the bishop's fare in the ancient chapel of a miserable refectory, was presented with a tumbledown bed in a tent surrounded by apple trees and weeds near the grillwork fence of a school for mongoloid boys, Dalai Lamas down from the snows of Tibet to learn in Lixbon how to mold little sheep out of modeling clay with the patience of novices. The chambermaids, who'd neglected to transfer to another clinic in the meantime, behaved toward us the same as they had toward the expelled patients, taking our temperature in the morning and at night, sternly forcing us under the sheets, and taking us walking after lunch in our bathrobes through a garden with bald camellias and basalt tanks from whose cracks hyacinth tresses were sprouting. In the sanatorium the days grew slower than a game of chess; the obligatory naps in canvas porch chairs with a tube of mercury stuck under the tongue and the branch of a plane tree tormenting feet were similar to weeks of calm seas, and some mulattoes, infected by the bruising sunsets and the perpetual autumn of mimosas, took to spitting up blood into enamel basins with a languid agony that the Mongoloids from Tibet, all identical like a nest of twins, would spy upon with secret wisdom from the gate.

Immediately after dawn a concert of throat clearing and bronchitis smothered the twittering of the birds in the garden and the footsteps of the doctors in the halls as they came to listen with their stethoscopes to the worsening in the thoraxes of the patients whose lungs were like the doilies under glass tabletops, ready to dissolve into clots with the mere force of a look. The man named Luís, who in spite of the absence of any symptoms was obliged to wear the bathrobe of a dying man, received permission for a period of an hour outside the hospital walls, escorted by an attendant who carried the porcelain chamber pot destined for the hemoptysis bacillae that were late in coming. In that way, in his slippers, he got to know the neighborhood that had been poisoned by the sanatorium and its sad miasmas and where the people, out of fear of contagion, had taken to pressing handkerchiefs against their mouths, giving the epicist the feeling that he was walking in his pajamas in the midst of a throng of aberrant surgeons dressed as fishwives, plumbers, or bank clerks, overwhelmed by the flaming lacquer of August.

More and more Lixbon was taking on the form of an aimless swirl of houses, a cavalcade of drainpipes, hedges, church spires, and streets whose sewer guts were exposed by repairs under a sky bursting with pustule clouds. In the midst of such hateful clarity that deprived people of the mercy of their own shadows, the writer, dazzled by the light, always followed by the fellow with the pot, ended up accompanying the false guilt of some funeral waiting for the night of cemetery cedars where the deceased evaporated under miniatures of Greek temples and plaster children, smothered by artificial flowers that smelled like the gauze cherries on hats and which he confused with the naphthaline smell of death. Sitting on the tiles of the edge of a row of tombs, with the basin within range of the first spit, he witnessed the modest cortege of poor people's funerals, that is, a coffin on a broken-down cart, old people stumbling behind, and stray dogs attracted by the presence of the corpse. Interned in a sanatorium far from the sea, he would have forgotten Loanda and the long-legged birds of the bay, necks sticking out from the top of palm trees, if in his tent, smack up against the building where the Dalai Lamas were learning diphthongs, he didn't sometimes hear, carried by the breath of the wind, the whisper of the engines of frigates going off to fish, leaving the Cabo Ruivo docks under the liturgical flames of the steel works.

On Sundays a flautist interned in the infirmary on the third floor, from where the airport radar and Seixal in the distance could be seen, would enliven the recreation room and its warped Ping-Pong tables and long concubine sofas with songs from the thirties secreted by the instrument's emphysema. He'd been a cook in a restaurant in Lobito frequented by black truckers and penniless drunks, and he would interrupt the insomniac aura of the television programs to exhume his fife from a satin case, put the three pieces that it was composed of together, pout his lips into a baby's suckle, rest his fingertips on the openings that were like the holes in a belt, and, on tiptoe with an aim to give more feeling to the notes, he would blow a tango of Gardel's through the pipe's pores, to which the coughing of the colonials gave a discordant accompaniment. During one of those painful recitals, right after the news of strikes by Swiss watchmakers, papal moon landings, and floods on the Cape Verde Islands, the man named Luís, who thought he was alone in a wicker easy chair, meditating on his octaves and composing glorious epi-sodes, noticed the presence beside him of a nearsighted albino fellow with a flask for expectoration on his knees, whom the sound of the flute was passing through without touching him, since tuberculosis and the loss of country had turned his body into a kind of marrow without substance. From time to time he would dribble a little thread of blood into the neck of the bottle that would coagulate into a little scarlet flower and he would disappear inside his pajamas again, reduced to a twinkling of eyes. At the end of the concert, nearly touching the floor with his drill pants, he would head off to a tent more recent than the others set up behind the main building, sixty or seventy feet from the kitchen in whose rooms the last odors of the diet broth were finally growing pale.

On following afternoons, as he made his way shuffling along through a web of coughing for his daily stroll, he would run into the nearsighted fellow, whose translucency made him blend in with the watercolors on the walls, collapsed in a canvas chair contemplating the apple trees in the garden or conversing on a corner of the veranda in mysterious conspiracies with gentle-men as nonexistent as he, each with his flask for spitting up roses in his hand and whose scarred tongues showed the inescapable mark of scurvy. Around that time the sanatorium got its first dead from among the skinniest returnees, tiny under the sheets that covered their heads, and we watched them go, laid out on a kind of tray with wheels, to the wine cellar for autopsies, a cloister where a butcher in a rubber apron and medlar-colored laundry gloves dissected intestines and arteries as he sliced with a big knife.

The man named Luís had already had a third of the poem written on the September afternoon when the captious myopic, after an hour of prudent vulture circling, tugged at his pajama sleeve and invited him to Ericeira to witness the landing of the king in the first week in October.

"Dom Sebastião will appear out of the waves on a white horse," he whistled, depositing a rose into his bottle.

The poet pictured a horde of consumptives in hospital uniforms, crouching in the mist of the dunes, waiting for a laughable monarch who would rise up out of the waters accompanied by his defeated army. Ever since he'd returned from Africa, even the flow of time had seemed absurd to him, and he still hadn't got used to the slow quince-jelly summer sunsets, the lack of grass with its avid insect rustle, and he would move about the city as if on a planet created by the mechanics of imagination, keeping informed through items in the newspapers that were as enigmatic as the singing of whales. So he accepted the invitation to the expedition in the same way that he accepted the pneumothoraxes and syrups of the doctors in the hospital who would pounce on him on Tuesdays and Fridays with a curative zeal of needles and tinctures of iodine.

"The only problem," the transparent gentleman warned him, without moving his lips, designating with his chin the orderlies who watched over the colonials' expectorations, "is Spanish informers."

And he explained that the country had been occupied by the Castilians as a consequence of the failure of the expedition to Morocco and the Prior of Crato, son of the prince Dom Luís, whose troops had deserted after two or three quick skirmishes and who was wandering about up north disguised as a pekingese, looking in vain for support in remote villages.

The details of the plan for the restoration of independence put forth by the patriot with the flute in the midst of attacks of bronchitis would be revealed to him during the naps after lunch or the almost daily wakes in the hospital chapel, decorated with heavy-lashed Saint Roques who contemplated, with pimpish piety, the tuberculars in double-breasted jackets, their mouths still open in an airless quaff. A hospital bookkeeper, bribed by the amorous maneuvers of a passionate mulatto woman who was redeeming herself in that way for twenty years of unbridled prostitution, had hired a bus with smoked-glass windows of the kind used for shepherding tourists through confinement towers, cathedrals, and insignificant things of that nature, which was to carry the patients to Ericeira to meet the faggot king and his tatterdemalion general staff, leaving from there to occupy the airport, radio and television stations, parliament, the bridge over the Tagus, and the entrances to Lixbon while platoons of internees from various hospitals under the command of people dying from serum, coughing up their petals of blood, would invade police headquarters, ministries, and docks, imprisoning the Spanish dukes in the fort at Caxias or piling them into rudderless schooners to drift in an ocean full of tritons.

The sanatorium existed through the following weeks in the ominous silence that precedes the flu and startles dogs, whose eyes turn purple from the sweat of fright. Consumption was decimating whole tents and the bodies, covered with numbered blankets, awaited the autopsy shears not only on the marble tables for quartering the deceased but on the steps leading down to the cellar themselves, on the threadbare rugs of the dining room, in the space for doctors' secretaries' legs, and behind kitchen stoves, along with newspapers and cockroaches, glowing from the coals of ovens. Some orderlies and doctors were already hiding incipient pharyngitis with the palms of their hands and showing up for work with dark circles under their eyes from nights of poor sleep, tormented by the agitation of fever. In the meantime, the flautist went on with his impassive concerts in spite of the dim glow of the television set, playing boleros with a vehemence that brought his audience to the point of tears as they drooled their ailments into their flasks while outside, the blasts of September dried the trees and gilded the almost autumn nights with thin yellow-gold dust. The man named Luís thought he caught the Morse code of the blond boy's followers in the fluctuation of the music, mainly when the musician, whom inspiration was freeing from the weight of his earthly state, rose up vertically into the air toward the stucco of the ceiling, moving his feet like the fins of a fish in a bowl over the chairs of the audience, returning to the floor with the last note, as light-footed as an acrobat. Going through the garden after the boleros were over, he imagined Spanish ships foundered on Baltic reefs and galleys off course and aground on the crags of the Ivory Coast in which hundreds of soldiers in armor moldy from demented storms were vainly waving at the edge of the forest where clusters of starstruck blacks were gathering.

During the soirée in which the musician replaced his usual repertory with the national anthem played in *paso-doble* time in order to fool the orderlies, very few colonists had survived the lung bacilli, judging from the empty benches and the smell of decomposed flesh in the infirmaries, and several doctors had left the hospital in search of better positions in clinics in the Alps, chilled by the moans of cuckoos. He was getting ready to get up from the sofa, nauseous from the pestilence of the dead, when the transparent fellow gently dragged him out to the brick terrace, which the roots of the apple trees were breaking up with an immense resurrective force, and pointed with his pinky, which was scarcely any different from the mallow color of the air, to a van with its lights on parked by the gate and consumptives in pajamas who were spread out through the thickets, on tiptoe, trying not make any noise in the silence of the darkness where they skated like deep-sea divers toward the coagulated lights of the vehicle.

The van was a stupendous car for rich Americans, with seats like barber's chairs, air-conditioning, airplane lavatories, individual earphones for zarzuelas and operas, and uniformed hostesses at a counter where they served biscuits and glasses of juice. The motor was running with the imperceptible hum of static electricity and for the last time the man named Luís looked at the immense hospital building composed of successive balconies and surrounded by indecipherable trellises displayed under the half-orange of the the moon. He saw the tents amidst the pattern of boxwoods, the laboratory where the fear of guinea pigs squeaked, and the mortuary filled with chitinous mummies like caimans in a museum. In the doctors' rooms from time to time the candlesticks of the physicians' insomniac navigation would slip along as they came down half-naked to the medicine cabinet in search of the corked bottle of hypnotics. The Dalai Lamas' school was a ship from whose hold flocks of bats with cruel canine teeth like French language teachers noiselessly surged. Carousels with ponies and other instruments of torture spun about in a kind of herd, meant to smash labels and open up heads, which the neighborhood pharmacist would lovingly suture with the help of a clamp. The man named Luís made himself comfortable on the upholstery, closed his eyes, and was already dreaming of the twisted alleys of Cazenga and military-police jeeps skidding in the treacherous mud, when the flautist, up in front with the fife in one hand and his spittle jar in the other, bellowed Saint George for Portugal. The pneumothorax hospice disappeared behind him, the shadows of buildings ran along in back of me through the tinted windows, the lampposts of the villas of Lumiar, covered with bougainvilleas up to the peepholes in the attic, had been left behind us with their silver sage and their canopied beds and all that was left was the loudspeaker on the bus that kept shrieking out military marches and communist poems.

They took the Sintra highway, following behind the exhaust of a vegetable truck that was whistling out war gases through all the pores of its broken-down engine, while several revolutionaries in pajamas fell into interminable coughing attacks and the transparent gentleman, a thermometer in his mouth, shuddered with fever on my left, awash in the ooze of his sweat. Rows of pine trees threatened us from the berms near the shadowy arch of the Queluz turnoff, devoured by the greed of the ivy. A hedge that ran parallel to the pavement disappeared suddenly, leaving us in a grove of spruce trees. Traffic policemen with luminous batons, lying in wait at crossroads, were giving out tickets to unwary calèches. The restaurants and the monuments of Sintra, dissolved in a perpetual mist and outlined by stadium footlights, squatted in the depth of the dampness with snooks coming and going through the open windows, leaving bluish reflections behind. The train station filled up at night with marigolds of missing people and the homes with roofs like the horns of Minho oxen, sailors in profile, floated with the laze of seaweed. The man named Luís remembered the concrete sunsets of Loanda, where everything looked exactly like what it was, without any nautical mysteries or footsteps of absent sirens, that were limited to conversations in hotel bars, a cigarette in scaly fingers, with aging Belgian women whom the fourth glass of port transformed.

The stretch from Sintra to Ericeira was made up of a desperation of curves and countercurves with clusters of hamlets along the way, country homes, émigrés' places, and drowsy dogs with black palates barking with hate by tavern doors. They passed the Mafra convent, full of centipedes and soldiers, and they reached Ericeira a little before three-twenty in the morning, their bones creaking with cold in their hospital pajamas, each with his expectoration bottle beneath his mouth and the breakfast pills in his pocket, under the command of the tubercular with the fife, whose asthma was whistling like a mournful set of bellows. They wandered through alleyways and small squares, recognizing one another by the tone of their throat clearing, sniffing with the clam-colored noses of sick people for the direction of the sea and the location of the beach, and flopping down onto terrace chairs, public benches missing slats, barriers that cut off a view of the water, granite walls fifty yards long, fishermen's canoes, rolled-up nets, glimmering buoys, and the wooden frames from canopies of a summer gone by that left its trash stuck in the dunes.

It was an old man with eyes trampled down by the advance of the bacilli, with a scarf around his kale-stem neck, who found the stairs with precarious landings that led down to the sand, and he called the musician, who was deciphering the mercury in his thermometer in the darkness in order to discover the centigrade of his misfortune. The transparent patriot and two or three more heroes with basins at their chins gathered together the tuberculars, who were wandering in bathrobes through a deserted parking lot, feeling out the possible direction of the ocean, which they spotted at the same time from all sides with its smell of acalephs and narcissuses, and in a flock, an uncertain herd of skeletons, they finally stumbled down the steps leading to the beach and the baskets of lowly sardines alongside a café with a gray cat sleeping on the uneven edge of the parapet.

Leaning on one another to share the appearance of the king on horseback with scars from slashes on his shoulders and stomach, they sat down on the randomly anchored boats, on the poop decks of trawlers, on cork floats, and on forgotten crates that gave off the smell of suicides, given to the dunes by the swirl of the currents. We waited, shivering in the morning breeze, for the glass sky of the first moments of light, the serge-colored mist of the equinox, the frieze of foam that would take us, mixed in with the marketplace flotsam of the waves and the lamb bleats of the water on the rocks' siphon, for a blond adolescent with a crown on his head and sulky lips, coming from Alcácer-Quibir with copper bracelets forged by the Gypsies of Carcavelos and cheap necklaces from Tangier around his neck, and all we could see as we squeezed the thermometers under our armpits and obediently spat our blood into the test tubes was the empty ocean, all the way to the horizon covered at intervals by a row of vinegar cruets, families of late summer people camping on the beach and fishing captains, pants rolled up, who looked uncomprehendingly at our band of gulls in bathrobes, perched on rudders and propellers, coughing, waiting, to the sound of a flute muted by the bowels of the sea, for the whinny of an impossible horse.